WALDORF AND THE SLEEPING GRANNY

Frieda Hughes

S I M O N   &   S C H U S T E R

LONDON • SYDNEY • NEW YORK • TOKYO • SINGAPORE • TORONTO

By the same author:

The Meal a Mile Long

First published in Great Britain in 1990
by Simon & Schuster Young Books

Photoset in North Wales by
Derek Doyle & Associates, Mold, Clwyd
Printed and bound in Great Britain at
The Guernsey Press

Simon & Schuster Young Books
Simon & Schuster Ltd
Wolsey House, Wolsey Road
Hemel Hempstead HP2 4SS

British Library Cataloguing in Publication Data

Hughes, Frieda
    Waldorf and the sleeping granny.
    I. Title
    823'.914 [J]

ISBN 0 7500 0301 4
ISBN 0 7500 0308 1 Pbk

For my husband, Clive,
with love

Chapter One

Ophelia shut the wooden gate at the bottom of the garden and looked up at the house. Mary Cage was watching her from the spare bedroom window with a smile on her lips, standing slightly to one side as though half her bulk was any less obvious than all of it.

All the way to the corner Ophelia could feel Mary Cage's eyes burning into her back, before she turned off towards the church.

She sat on the churchyard wall facing a row of empty terraced houses across the quiet street, and let out a sigh of relief. No one lived behind the broken windows and doors with their peeling paint; here she didn't have to put on a brave face because there was no one to see her. Not like at home, where Mary had been watching Ophelia ever since she had moved in with Ophelia and her grandmother.

"We need a housekeeper," Ophelia's granny had said, glaring angrily at the plaster-cast on her leg. In the middle of painting the upstairs windowsills she had slipped and fallen badly; now her broken leg was immobilised in a heavy plaster-cast and she couldn't get about at all.

Only one person had answered the advert in the local paper for a temporary housekeeper: fat, dirty Mary Cage.

When Mary arrived on the doorstep, she looked Grandmother in the eye and announced she could start work immediately. To Ophelia's astonishment, Grandmother let her in.

From that moment, Mary kept Ophelia away from her grandmother. The only time Ophelia could see the old lady was when the Doctor called. The last time had been two days ago. Mary had been with them for only a week, and already the house was hers.

An old yellow car drove past the churchyard, breaking the silence. It was going too fast and had too many people in it, all crushed up against the windows. The car slowed down, one of the back doors opened and a bundle was thrown into the street. Ophelia jumped off the wall and shouted to the people in the car that they had dropped something, but the car didn't stop.

The bundle twitched. Ophelia watched it with growing apprehension and realised it was alive. For a moment it remained crumpled in the middle of the road, then it struggled painfully to its feet and became an enormous dog. Who would do that to a dumb animal? The dog stood, swaying slightly and staring after the last spluttering exhaust cloud, and Ophelia could see how his fur was long and matted and his ears drooped. Surely the owners would come back for him? Then Ophelia swallowed hard as she realised the car door opening like that had been no accident.

With unsteady legs the dog lurched up to the pavement. Then he saw Ophelia. For a second his eyes widened and his shoulders quivered with fear: he was terrified. Ophelia sat back on the wall as if to show she wasn't interested, and the dog seemed reassured. He stumbled towards her, his huge head lowered and his watery eyes fixed on her face.

If Mary wasn't home, she could take the dog back with her and look after it. She'd always wanted a dog, but Mary's presence had changed everything and Ophelia was having enough trouble just looking after herself.

The dog sat gingerly on the pavement at Ophelia's feet. Ophelia felt terrible – she

couldn't take the dog home with her, and she didn't want to leave him all alone.

"You must stay here," she told him helplessly. "I'm sure they'll be back for you later." The dog looked up at her. Ophelia could have sworn she saw him shake his head. Then she quickly climbed off the wall and hurried home.

"I wish I could have him," she muttered angrily, tears burning her eyelids. "I'd look after him properly, if only – if only I could take him home with me." She nearly turned back, but then she remembered Mary's leering face and her sick grandmother, sleeping so strangely now.

SLEEPING GRANNY

On the way back to the house Ophelia had to walk past the Doctor's. She stood outside his gate and wondered if she should go in. If only she had a friend she could talk to about it, but school had broken up and everyone was away for the holidays. Besides, everyone at school thought Ophelia was odd, though Ophelia could never understand why; after all, she looked like they did and dressed like they did. Her ordinary face and long brown hair were hardly unusual.

Ophelia concluded that Doctor Wolf was the only person she could talk to. If only she could make him believe what she had to say.

The Doctor's wife let her in. Ophelia wished someone more like Mrs Wolf had answered her grandmother's advert, instead of Mary Cage.

Mrs Wolf was a plumpish, pleasant lady in her mid-fifties, with curly grey hair and nervous fingers. She always looked as though she was in the middle of the housework because she never took off her flowered apron, and her sleeves were always rolled up to her elbows.

Mrs Wolf showed Ophelia into the Doctor's study, where she was to wait until he'd finished surgery in the room down the hall. Ophelia sat, dwarfed in an enormous leather chair in front of an enormous oak desk. Everything was big here, like the Doctor himself.

She just had time to take in the dark blue walls and carpet, the shelves of books, all with red leather binding and gold lettering, the large cannonball that propped the door open, and the highly polished brass microscope that stood on the end of the desk, when Doctor Wolf appeared in the doorway with Mrs Wolf hovering at his shoulder. He sent his wife off to get them some tea and pulled another chair up to Ophelia's.

"I understand there's something personal you wanted to talk to me about," he said, smiling and stroking down the few strands of hair left on the back of his bald head. "Something that couldn't be dealt with by a visit to my surgery."

Ophelia nodded, beginning to wish she hadn't come. If she went home now, she'd probably find things weren't as bad as she imagined.

"It's about Mary, our new housekeeper," she began hesitantly.

"Go on," said Doctor Wolf softly. "Just take your time."

"Mary really doesn't like me, and I'm sure you won't believe me but she's making life miserable. She doesn't like me being in the house and she won't let me visit Gran, except when you're there. She puts on a show for you."

Gripping the arms of her chair, Ophelia explained in her most serious voice how Gran was only awake during his visits, and how she now wanted to sleep continually. "For all I know she might have been asleep since you last called," explained Ophelia, "because I haven't been allowed to see her and I haven't heard a sound from her room."

"Sleep does help the healing process," Doctor Wolf told her, "though it's ridiculous that you are prevented from seeing your own grandmother, when all she's got is a broken leg."

"Please, Doctor, won't you have another look at her? You've never known me to complain about anything that wasn't real, have you?"

The Doctor shook his head and had to admit that if Ophelia had ever said she was ill, she most certainly was.

"Well, now I'm complaining for Gran, because she can't complain for herself."

They were interrupted by Mrs Wolf bringing in the tea tray. She poured tea for two and left them alone again.

Between biscuits the Doctor agreed that he would visit Ophelia's grandmother again tomorrow, paying special attention to Mary's behaviour.

"Why not come now?" Ophelia wanted to know.

The Doctor paused for a moment. "Yes, why not now," he agreed.

"Actually," said Ophelia, struck by a sudden thought, "if you come and see her now, will you just give me time to get home first? You know, sort of separate from you?"

"So it doesn't look as though you've come to get me, is that it?" Doctor Wolf smiled. Ophelia nodded. "You really *are* frightened of Mary, aren't you?" he said seriously. "Well, if your grandmother really is as bad as you say she is, we can have her taken into hospital. You could come and stay here with me and Mrs Wolf if you wanted to, and I could drive you in to visit her every day."

"That would be wonderful of you!" cried Ophelia. "And if Gran isn't at home, then there's no reason for Mary to be there either."

She left without finishing her tea. For the first time in the week since Mary had arrived, she ran home.

As she got near the garden gate, she could see something sitting there, on the pavement. She slowed to a trot, worried in case it was ...

well, anything to do with Mary.

The thing got to its feet and turned, from what looked like a bundle of old jumpers, into a dog. Ophelia suddenly realised it was *the* dog. "How did you know where I lived?" she asked out loud, trying to get past it. The dog stood in her way and whimpered.

"Oh, please, not now," wailed Ophelia in exasperation, "I have to get in. Besides, if your owners find out where you are, they'll say I've stolen you."

Ophelia squeezed through the garden gate and shut the dog out, but it scratched on the gate and whimpered, more plaintively this time.

Ophelia glanced at the spare bedroom window and saw with relief that Mary wasn't watching. "Go home," she told the dog firmly. The dog sat down and wagged its hairy tail. She turned her back and it began scratching at the gate again.

Ophelia hesitated for a moment. No one who was responsible enough to own a dog would let it get into such a state; not only was he filthy and tangled, but his matted fur clung to his skinny sides and Ophelia knew his bones would be sticking out underneath.

A flea bounced down the dog's nose and fell

off the end. "It wouldn't do you any harm to have a proper meal, I suppose," said Ophelia reluctantly. The dog stopped whining and grinned up at Ophelia. He stood on his hind legs and for a second Ophelia thought he was going to lick her face. But instead he reached over the gate and hooked his paw under the latch. The gate, and Ophelia's mouth, swung open.

Mary wasn't in the kitchen when Ophelia got there. Quickly, she opened the fridge door. All she could find was a half-empty tin of beans, which she scooped into a saucer, but the dog seemed to love them.

"I don't know what we'll eat tomorrow," she told him, "I had the rest of them last night, because Mary won't cook for me; and there doesn't seem to be anything else."

The sound of heavy footsteps on the stairs announced Mary's impending arrival. The kitchen door swung open just as the dog slid under the table. The animal had wonderfully sharp instincts.

"So you're back!" snapped Mary ungraciously.

"How's Gran?" asked Ophelia, not expecting a sensible answer.

"Sleeping, as she should be if she wants her leg to heal quickly. I advise you not to try and wake her. She found it difficult enough to get off to sleep as it was, without being woken by you."

"Couldn't I just look in on her?" pleaded Ophelia. "I'll only stand in the doorway."

Mary put the empty soup bowl she was carrying in to the sink, on top of two or three other soup bowls from earlier in the day and several from the day before.

"Not a chance," she told Ophelia.

"Is there anything I can eat then?" said Ophelia, changing the subject.

"There are some beans in the fridge," Mary replied.

"I just ate them," Ophelia confessed, "but I'm still hungry."

"So buy some food then. I don't have time to look after the house and your grandmother *and* go shopping. Besides, your grandmother shouldn't be left without qualified attention for a moment. Why don't you go and buy something?"

"I don't have any money," Ophelia pointed out.

"Well," said Mary scornfully, "neither do I, until your grandmother's well enough to pay me."

"How are you going to feed *her* then?"

"I have all I need for her home-made soup," retorted Mary.

"And what will you eat?" asked Ophelia.

"Soup," replied Mary.

"So why can't I eat soup too?' Ophelia demanded.

Mary looked at her strangely for a moment. Then she smiled.

"Yes, why can't you," she said evenly. "I suppose I think of it as being for your grandmother. But it won't do you any harm to have a few extra vitamins. For the moment, though, why don't I see if I can find a few biscuits and we'll have them with a cup of tea."

Ophelia could hardly believe her ears. Mary was making an effort to be friendly – but why?

Did this mean she shouldn't have called on the Doctor?

She was sitting at the table, about to drink her tea and eat the last two boring biscuits, when the Doctor arrived. Mary left the kitchen to answer the door.

As soon as Mary had gone, the dog emerged from beneath the table, looked up at Ophelia and shook his head. "What's wrong with you?" she asked him. He shook his head again. Ophelia shrugged her shoulders and raised her cup to her lips. The dog stood on his hind legs and batted it from her hand, leaving her holding only the handle, then disappeared under the table again.

Quickly, Ophelia cleared up the mess, scolding the dog under her breath as she did so. "Your owners probably kicked you out for anti-social behaviour," she muttered.

The kitchen door stood ajar and Ophelia heard Mary exclaim pleasantly, "Why, Doctor Wolf, what a surprise! I didn't think we'd be seeing you again until next week."

"Just passing," came the Doctor's reply, "and since Edith is one of my favourite patients, I thought I wouldn't be doing my duty if I didn't call in at the slightest excuse, now that she actually needs me for once."

"Oh, I'm sorry," she heard Mary say, "but she's only just gone off to sleep and I'd hate to disturb her."

"I'm sure she won't mind being woken when she knows it's me," said Doctor Wolf firmly, "and it's still quite early in the day to be in bed, even if her leg *is* in plaster." Ophelia could imagine the fixed smile on his face as he manoeuvred his black bag past Mary's bulk. Now he was in the hallway. Ophelia glanced at the dog to make sure he was still cowering under the table, and went out to join them. She could swear the dog winked at her as she left.

"Hello, Ophelia!" cried Doctor Wolf with obvious pleasure. "Nice to see you again. You should call round for tea one afternoon while your grandmother's recovering. It might give Mary a break from having to look after the two of you."

"Did you drink your tea, Ophelia?" demanded Mary. "Why don't you go and finish it?"

"I spilt it," Ophelia told her, and was puzzled by the strange expression that crossed Mary's face.

The Doctor took the stairs two at a time. Ophelia was about to follow when Mary caught her by the arm, her nails biting into Ophelia's flesh. "You went to get him, didn't you, you stupid brat! You're so worried about your precious grandmother, you couldn't wait to tell ridiculous tales all over town, could you? What did you say to get him here?"

"But I didn't get him here," protested Ophelia, just loud enough for the Doctor to hear and realise what she was being questioned about. If Mary had nothing to hide, why should she be so angry?

"This room is locked," announced the Doctor as he tried the handle of Grandmother's bedroom door.

Hurriedly, Mary pulled a key from the pocket of her dirty white apron and opened the door. "It's just to make sure Ophelia doesn't creep in and disturb her," she explained.

Ophelia was surprised how much paler her grandmother had grown in only two days. Her skin was stretched over her bones like thin white cotton, and her breathing was inaudible. And the room smelt bad: dry and stale.

Doctor Wolf hurried to the side of the bed. "Edith," he said gently, placing his bag on the floor. "Edith?" But the old woman didn't stir. He lifted her wrist and felt her pulse. There was an urgency about his movements now.

"Is she all right?" asked Ophelia, panic rising in her throat.

"Of course she's all right, you silly child," snapped Mary. "She had a bowl of hot soup only half an hour ago. It helped her get off to sleep."

"Just what was in your soup?" asked the Doctor, lifting one of Grandmother's eyelids and staring into the iris.

"Vegetables and herbs," Mary told him. "Lots of vitamins. I make it especially for her. A hot liquid drink works wonders if you want to feel drowsy."

"This isn't drowsy," said the Doctor accusingly, confirming Ophelia's terrible sense of forboding. Then he slapped Grandmother's face a couple of times, gently, and called her name, but the old woman's head just lolled sideways on the pillow.

"Edith!" shouted the Doctor suddenly, shaking her by the shoulders until Ophelia thought Grandmother's head would roll off the side of the bed.

"You must have given her something to make her like this! This is not a normal sleep," said the Doctor angrily.

"I tell you," said Mary again, "she's had nothing but harmless vegetable soup. In fact, since Ophelia and I are going to have the same soup for supper, why don't you try some too and see for yourself how harmless it is?" Her voice was sharp with resentment.

The doctor hesitated. Then he said, "Yes, Mary, I'd like to stay for supper. You could start making it now, while I try to make Edith a little more comfortable."

Mary realised she was dismissed and left, casting a poisonous look over her shoulder at Ophelia as she went.

"You're not actually going to *eat* her soup, are you?" Ophelia wanted to know.

"It's all right." Doctor Wolf smiled grimly. "It can't be poisoned, but I may be able to tell just what kind of herbs are in it. Mary might have added something by accident." Ophelia doubted whether anything Mary did was accidental but said nothing. "And I'll call an ambulance, because your grandmother has become far too weak to stay here."

"Doctor Wolf, is that you?" came a thin, feeble voice.

"Gran!" cried Ophelia. "You're awake!"

"Yes, I'm here," said Doctor Wolf.

"I'm so *tired* all the time," the old lady complained.

"Mary keeps saying you can't sleep," said Ophelia.

"Oh, I can sleep," said Grandmother weakly.

"I just wish I could stay awake for longer than it takes to eat a bowl of Mary's soup."

"Please Gran, tell Mary to go; then we can look after you," begged Ophelia. But Grandmother was already asleep again.

"Don't worry," said Doctor Wolf, leading Ophelia from the room. "When your grandmother goes into hospital, and you come and stay with us, Mary will have no reason to stay here."

Downstairs, they found Mary stirring the soup. "I'll just use your phone, if I may," said the Doctor briskly and disappeared into the living room before Mary could answer.

"Drat!" she snapped. "I was just about to tell him it's been cut off. I don't think your grandmother can have paid the bill. Go and tell him, would you?"

Ophelia found the Doctor staring with a puzzled expression at the telephone receiver. "It's totally dead," he announced. Ophelia was about to repeat what Mary had told her when, for no reason she could explain, she picked up the trailing telephone wire and followed it to the wall, where she found the wire had been cut close to the socket. She held up the trailing end for Doctor Wolf to see.

"She said it had been cut off," she explained.

The Doctor grunted. "I don't think we should tell her we know the real reason why it doesn't work. We must get your grandmother out of here first."

"Couldn't we call the police?" asked Ophelia.

The Doctor shook his head. "What would we tell them? That we have a sick old lady who can't stay awake, a fat woman who cuts phone wires and a pan full of home-made soup?" Ophelia saw what he meant.

"I'll phone the hospital from home," he said,

"when I've had a chance to try out this soup of Mary's."

The soup was oily and green. Mary sat the Doctor and Ophelia down at the table and served them a bowl each. Ophelia dropped her spoon so she could peer under the table. The dog had gone.

"Aren't you having some?" she asked.

"There was only enough for two," Mary answered. "I'll make myself some more later." She turned her back for a moment and the Doctor sniffed the thick mess before him, then tried a little. It clung to the spoon like glue, and didn't drip so much as ooze and stretch. Ophelia watched him with distaste.

"Actually, it tastes fine," whispered the Doctor in surprise.

"Of course it does," cried Mary, overhearing. "It might *look* strange, but it's the flavour and goodness that count. Come on, Ophelia, try some before it gets cold."

Ophelia glanced at the Doctor, who didn't appear to be suffering any ill effects. She lifted a spoonful of the mess to her nose. It smelt a little sweet and rather nice. She was just about to put it in her mouth when there was a violent banging at the kitchen window, and a voice shouted, "*No! Don't eat!*" Ophelia dropped her spoon in surprise.

"Who's that, prowling around outside?" demanded Mary, storming to the kitchen door and throwing it open. Her voice died away in her throat. "There's no one there," she said.

She was just about to shut the door when the strange dog pushed in past her.

"What's that filthy animal doing in here?" she screeched.

"He followed me home earlier today," Ophelia told her. "And there's nothing you can do to stop me keeping him. Is there, Doctor Wolf?"

Doctor Wolf was about to reply when his eyes closed and he slumped forward on to his arms, his elbow in his soup. Ophelia shook his shoulder, but he wouldn't sit up. "What have you done to him?" she demanded. "It's the soup, isn't it?"

Mary smoothed down her dirty apron and walked out. "Clean up, there's a good girl," she said over her shoulder. "Oh, and don't wake the Doctor. He's obviously been overworking."

"Wake up!" cried Ophelia, shaking the Doctor uselessly. She was crying with fear and frustration – who would help her now?

"Whoever was outside knew the soup was dangerous," she said under her breath. She ran out into the garden and the dog followed her, but there was no one there; there wasn't even a footprint in the flowerbed beneath the kitchen window – only dog prints. Ophelia looked down at the animal. "Well, it couldn't have been you." She sighed. "If only you could talk, I expect you'd be able to tell me who it was."

The smell that arose from the dustbin, when Ophelia opened the lid to throw away the soup, was like rotting cabbage and clung to the back of her throat. In the bottom of the bin were the remains of some strange plants, with purple pods and yellow-spotted leaves. One of the pods twitched slightly as Ophelia scraped the sticky soup out of the bowls on top of it. "That must be what she makes the soup from," she told the dog.

She put the bowls in the sink and saw that the ones from earlier in the day were already growing mould with bright orange spores. "Nothing could grow that quickly!" she gasped. The dog arrived at her side, put his paws on the edge of the sink and looked over. He shook his head.

She crouched down and rubbed his neck. "I could swear you think," she told him. "I ought to give you a name if you're going to stay here. But not an ordinary one, because I don't think you are an ordinary dog."

She got a book from the living room and opened it on the kitchen table beside the slumped figure of the Doctor. Holding a pencil, she shut her eyes, turned a few pages, then stabbed at the book. She opened her eyes and announced that it looked as though the dog was to be called "because". The dog stood on his hind legs, reached out a paw and pushed the pencil down the page until he was satisfied with its resting place. "*Waldorf*," Ophelia read out, "as in Waldorf Hotel. Well, if that's what you want. But look what you've done to Gran's book!" The dog beat his tail on the ground and drooled slightly.

Ophelia sighed and wiped her eyes. "Somehow, I have to wake up the Doctor, get Gran to hospital and get rid of Mary," she told Waldorf. "And I can't do any of it on my own. But the one thing I can do is give you a bath." Waldorf turned on his heels and trotted out of the room. "It won't hurt you!" Ophelia called after him.

She heard him bark from the bathroom, and found him already sitting in the bath. Astonished, Ophelia turned on the shower above him and began to soap him all over. Then she left him sitting there while she went

27

to get another towel. "Don't you dare shake yourself until I get back," she instructed, "or you'll get the bathroom soaked. I'll only be a couple of minutes."

Ophelia was gone less than a minute, but when she tried to open the bathroom door on her return she found it was stuck. "Hey, what's wrong?" she muttered, quietly, so Mary wouldn't hear her from the spare room. She pushed again, harder this time. Something jumped away from behind the door, but when Ophelia stepped into the bathroom, she found it wasn't Waldorf as she expected. It was a boy with long black hair and a wild look in his eyes. He was holding the hand towel around his waist and dripping all over the floor.

"How did you get in?" demanded Ophelia. "And where's Waldorf?" The boy didn't answer, but his mouth opened and closed as though he was fighting for words. Ophelia stepped forward. *"What have you done with him?"* The boy backed away. He was shivering and had a stricken look on his face. "Here," said Ophelia, handing him the towel she was carrying.

Hurriedly, the boy wrapped the big towel around the hand towel, then he looked down at Ophelia's feet and his eyes widened. He

pointed at them, his mouth struggling to get the words out. 'P...p...please," he said hoarsely, "you're standing on my skin."

"Skin?" Ophelia looked at the floor and saw she was standing on a crumpled heap of wet fur. She picked it up, and suddenly realised it was Waldorf's limp, wet coat, with flapping ears and empty eye holes.

"Aaaaaah!" she squealed, tossing it away from her. Quick as a flash, the boy scooped up the skin and clutched it tightly to his chest.

"You *are* Waldorf, aren't you?" said Ophelia accusingly.

The boy blushed and nodded. "I only took off my skin to wring it out, so I wouldn't get your floor wet." His hoarse voice was becoming clearer with every word he spoke.

"Would you like me to find you some clothes?" Ophelia asked him.

He shook his head. "I'm not really a boy ... Just a dog who can be human sometimes. I don't like wearing human clothes, because I still feel naked without my own skin. Please, if you turn around for a moment, I can put it on again."

Ophelia obligingly turned her back until he told her it was all right to look. He was just pulling the head of the skin over his own face.

Then he was Waldorf again, and only slightly damp. He'd even folded up the towels and placed them neatly on the side of the bath.

"Why didn't you talk earlier?" asked Ophelia curiously.

"Because usually I can only talk when my owner is a witch," he replied, "and you didn't look like a witch, so I didn't know I'd be able to."

"I'm not a witch," Ophelia told him.

The boy looked puzzled. "Then Mary must be," he said, "though usually the witch has to be my owner. That's the way it's always been. Climbing out of my skin goes with the power of speech."

"Mary can't be a witch," protested Ophelia, "because they don't exist."

"Neither do talking dogs," Waldorf pointed out. "In fact, I'm certain she's a witch, because only a witch knows how to make sleeping soup."

"Am I your new owner?" asked Ophelia hopefully.

"No one else is," Waldorf replied with a grin. "Anyway, you need help and I need a new home."

Waldorf, as it turned out, had a number of useful suggestions to make regarding Ophelia's predicament.

First, he dictated a message, "Wanted, good witch, urgently, please call at ...", giving the address and Ophelia's name.

"What's this for?" asked Ophelia curiously, as she printed the words on a small piece of paper.

"It's an advert for the local newspaper," replied Waldorf. "No one but a real witch will believe it. You need a good witch to get rid of a bad one, and Mary is certainly a bad witch."

He instructed Ophelia not to touch any food or drink Mary might give her. "She obviously wants to put you to sleep too," he said. "The thing that puzzles me is why, if she can't get you to eat her soup, she doesn't try something else. There are all sorts of things she could do to get you out of her way – which is where she would like you to be."

"Why would she want to do anything?"

"Because she's house-hunting," Waldorf explained. "An evil witch never has her own home; she's too lazy to work for one like other people. So she takes a home from somebody else. Of course the houses don't last long because of the way they're treated, and eventually they collapse."

Ophelia was horrified. She'd hoped things might not be as bad as she thought, but Waldorf was telling her they were actually worse.

He sent her off to the Doctor's house so she could use the phone to call an ambulance.

"And tell his wife that he'll be staying here for a couple of days to look after your grandmother, who's in a critical condition and can't be moved. But don't let her hear you calling the hospital, or she'll know you're lying."

Mrs Wolf was naturally concerned. "You must let me bring over one or two of the Doctor's things," she told Ophelia, her fingers twisting and untwisting in agitation. "He might need them, and perhaps I can cook a stew or soup or something, to help out."

"Er, um ... actually, we're all right for soup at the moment," said Ophelia. "As for the Doctor's things, I could take them home with me and save you a journey. But our phone is out of order and I have to call a friend, so perhaps I could use yours while you get them ready for me?" Ophelia was delighted with herself: it all sounded like such sense. Mrs Wolf disappeared upstairs to get whatever it was she thought Doctor Wolf should have with him.

As soon as she was alone, Ophelia called the hospital for an ambulance. She told them she was following Doctor Wolf's instructions, and that he couldn't come to the phone because he was with her grandmother, who was in a coma (it was the only medical term she could think of to describe her grandmother's condition).

Carrying the small overnight case Mrs Wolf had given her, containing the Doctor's toothbrush, pyjamas, shaving kit and a change of clothes, Ophelia called in at the office of the local newspaper and placed her advert.

To her relief they said they would send the bill later, though they thought the advert was extremely odd. "It's for my grandmother," Ophelia explained weakly and hurried home to wait for the ambulance.

Waldorf and Mary were in the kitchen. Waldorf was following Mary so closely she kept losing her balance every time she turned around. When she tried to kick him he jumped aside, then returned to his original position.

"Get this stupid flea-bitten dog out of here!" she screamed at the top of her voice as soon as she saw Ophelia.

"He's as entitled to be here as you are," retorted Ophelia. "I can't help it if he likes you."

She was watching Mary chopping something on the draining board when she suddenly realised it was a dead snake.

"When is the Doctor going to wake up?" she asked. "He can't stay here for ever. He has to see

his patients." She had hidden the Doctor's case behind a chair in the living room.

"He can stay where he is as long as it suits me," snapped Mary, trying to kick Waldorf away from her ankles. The Doctor let out a loud snore.

"What will happen if I tell people what you've done to him and my grandmother?"

"Who could you tell?" Mary laughed and

waved the snake's tail at Ophelia. "I know all about you and your grandmother: neither of you have any friends to tell! I was employed to look after your grandmother until she's well again, and until that time, there's nothing you can do."

"But she's not getting any better," protested Ophelia.

"I will leave only if she recovers," said Mary ominously.

Chapter Two

Ophelia and Waldorf sat despondently in Ophelia's room. They hadn't been able to see Grandmother because the door was locked again.

"At least we know why she picked on your house," said Waldorf with a sigh. "It's because you don't have people dropping round to visit you all the time."

"And we know that Gran isn't going to get any better," said Ophelia quietly, "unless we can get her out of here."

"If she hasn't been given too much soup already," muttered Waldorf. Ophelia didn't hear him because there was someone banging on the front door. She jumped to her feet. "Oh no, the ambulance is here. I should have waited downstairs!"

She raced downstairs, and found Mary calmly telling the two ambulance men that the call must have been a hoax.

"No it isn't!" shouted Ophelia. "*I* called you. It's my grandmother, please, you have to help her, she's upstairs." She was frantic, they just *had* to believe her.

The two men looked at each other as if they didn't know who to believe. "Look here, little girl," said one of them with exaggerated patience, "the lady here says there's no sick grandmother. Grown-ups are quite capable of telling whether someone needs us or not, you know."

Ophelia hated the condescending tone the man had used and she hated being called "little girl". She pulled herself up to her full height. "I know you don't believe me," she said, her voice quaking, "but sometimes strange things happen in people's houses, and some people treat other people badly but manage to hide it. There's no way you can be *sure* I'm not telling the truth, without coming to have a look."

"I suppose we'd be daft not to," one man said to the other.

"It won't hurt," said the other, and they followed Ophelia up the stairs. Mary stood at the bottom, her face expressionless.

"I'll have to call Mary to unlock the room for you," said Ophelia, "because she's keeping Gran a prisoner. She won't even let me visit her."

Ophelia reached the end of the corridor and her mouth fell open.

"Is the old lady in there?" asked one of the men, pointing to the door in front of them.

Ophelia shook her head. "That's Mary's room," she told him.

"Well, where *is* your grandmother's room then?" asked the man impatiently.

"It was here, next to Mary's room," Ophelia said weakly, "but it seems to have gone." She looked down at Waldorf for help, but he shrugged his shoulders apologetically to remind her he couldn't talk in front of others.

"I promise you, the door was here earlier," wailed Ophelia. "Oh no, I don't know what's happening!" She banged on the wall with both fists. "Gran, Gran, wake up, *say something*!" she shouted. If only her grandmother would speak, it would prove there was a room behind what was now a blank wall. "Gran, wake up!" she yelled again.

"Look!" she cried urgently, grabbing one of the men by the sleeve, "I'll show you!" She dragged him first to Mary's room. "You see how small this is?" she said. Then she dragged him into the bathroom, which was on the other side of Grandmother's invisible bedroom. "And you see how small this is?" she cried. The man nodded. "Well, what do you suppose is in between if it's not another room!"

"Look," he said gently, "I don't know what could be behind the wall, love, but if it were a room it would have a door and there is no door, and this wallpaper looks so old that I doubt someone came along just today and walled the door up."

Mary was waiting for the men at the bottom of the stairs. "I'm so sorry your time has been wasted," she said smugly. "I'll show you out."

Ophelia sat on the landing with her head in her hands. She could hear one of the ambulance men telling Mary how she must have her hands full with such a troublesome child.

"Wait!" shouted Ophelia suddenly. "Wait!" She ran downstairs and collided with the men as they stood in the hallway. "At least you can take the Doctor. He's in some sort of coma!" With more strength than she thought she possessed, Ophelia dragged one of the men into the kitchen, while his friend followed with Mary.

"There!" said Ophelia. "See for yourself, you try and wake him! No one can! He's been like that ever since lunchtime. It's the soup that did it."

The ambulance man shook the Doctor, lifted one of his eyelids and looked into his eye. He felt his pulse. Mary caught his eye and lifted an imaginary bottle to her lips. "Aaah," said the man knowingly. "Come on," he said to his companion, "there's nothing we can do for the Doctor here that a good sleep won't cure."

"But you don't understand!" wailed Ophelia. "It's not a natural sleep!"

"Oh, we know that!"laughed the men. They left without a backward glance.

"You'll have to be quicker than that to beat me," Mary said with a smirk when they had gone. Ophelia decided that Mary's filthy white apron and frilly pink satin shirt made her look like a decaying marshmallow.

"There's nothing you can do to get rid of me," said Mary, still smiling. "But I might just be able to get rid of you." Ophelia suspected this didn't mean her simply moving out.

"How are you going to feed Gran if there's no door to her room?" Ophelia demanded. "She has to eat, you know, or she'll die."

"Oh, she won't die," said Mary cheerfully.

"But she might fade, like a photograph in the sun. As for the door to her room, it was there all the time."

Ophelia ran upstairs, with Waldorf at her heels. The door was back again. Frantically, she turned and pulled at the round brass door handle, but it was still locked.

"What did she mean, Waldorf, when she said Grandmother might 'fade'?"

"She could be talking about a side effect of long-term soup-eating," said Waldorf thoughtfully. "She might be telling the truth about your grandmother not dying, but it might be possible for your grandmother to sleep herself into oblivion."

They waited in Ophelia's room for the sound of Mary's footsteps on the stairs. When Mary had gone into Grandmother's room Ophelia sprang into action. "Now we'll see if Grandmother wakes up when she's fed," she told Waldorf.

Peering through the keyhole of the bedroom door Ophelia was overwhelmed with despair. Out of force of habit, Mary had taken the key out of the other side of the door, so that Ophelia had a clear view of the bed. "Mary is spooning soup into Gran's mouth and Gran doesn't even have her eyes open," she whispered to Waldorf.

They crept back to her bedroom.

"Apart from anything else," muttered Ophelia, "we need to find a way to get something to eat ourselves. All you've had is baked beans, and I can't remember when I last ate. I'm starving."

Waldorf told her to relax. "This is where I can be really useful," he smiled. He left her then, and returned half an hour later with a carrier bag of shopping in his mouth.

In the middle of the night Ophelia was woken by the sound of the front door opening and closing. She climbed out of bed and peered through the window to see Mary squeezed into her grandmother's best coat, walking down the garden path to the gate.

Ophelia watched the gate until the sky turned grey and a soft mist began to form on the lawn. Suddenly, Mary emerged from the mist at the end of the path, carrying something.

"Waldorf!" Ophelia whispered urgently. "Wake up! Mary's brought something back, and there's someone with her."

A moment later he was at her side. "So that's when she collects those weeds," he growled. Then he saw her companion.

"Oh dear," he muttered. "Oh dear, this isn't good at all."

"Why? What on earth are you talking about? Who's down there?"

"That, my dear Ophelia, is Mary's familiar, though it's hard to tell whether it's male or female."

"Does that mean they know each other very well?"

"No, silly, it's usually an animal of some kind which can take on a human form, usually a cat or a dog," replied Waldorf. "A cat becomes a girl and a dog becomes a boy. I'm a familiar when I'm with a practising witch. This confirms that Mary is all I thought she was, and that she feels nothing can threaten her position here. All we can do is hope someone answers our advert very soon," he ended gloomily.

Ophelia lay on her bed in the dark, waiting for daylight: nothing ever seemed quite so bad in the daylight. Waldorf lay on the floor beside her. Neither of them could sleep. That was how they heard the soft footsteps on the landing. For a moment Ophelia thought Mary must be paying her grandmother another visit, but the footsteps came to a halt outside her own door. She held her breath as the handle turned gently. The door swung open and Waldorf shuffled sideways under the bed and out of sight.

"Good," she heard Mary whisper. "The dog isn't here and Ophelia's fast asleep."

"Eeeeow, that's good." The voice that answered was high-pitched.

Ophelia didn't know whether to sit up and face them or carry on pretending she was asleep. She decided to wait and see what happened.

Mary and her companion came and stood either side of the bed. Ophelia caught a shadowy glimpse of them through half-closed lids.

"*Now!*" shouted Mary. Ophelia tried to

struggle free of the hands that suddenly grabbed her, but she was too late. Mary hauled her into a kneeling position and held both her arms behind her back.

"Let me go!" screamed Ophelia. "Let me go!"

"Now pour the soup into her mouth," Mary shouted to the girl who stood on the other side of the bed. The girl took hold of Ophelia's hair in one hand and pulled her head back, until Ophelia couldn't shout any longer. The other hand held a jug of soup over Ophelia's open mouth and tilted it.

At that moment the bed heaved and Waldorf bounded out from beneath it. His powerful jaws opened and tore into the girl holding the jug. Soup went everywhere as the girl screamed and hissed and ran howling out of the room. Waldorf turned his attention to Mary, and she followed her familiar as fast as her fat legs would carry her.

Ophelia was left sobbing on the soup-stained bed. "There, there," whispered Waldorf, licking her hands. "I wasn't going to let them do anything to you. They've gone now, and they won't be back. I'll look after you." Ophelia threw her arms around his neck and buried her face in his fur.

"That was definitely a cat," mumbled

Waldorf. Ophelia sat back and stared at him. "It didn't look like a cat to me," she said.

"It smelt like one though," said Waldorf, "and did you hear her voice? Real cat vocal chords. The interesting thing is that Mary is trying to *force* you to take the sleeping soup, when there are a number of alternatives at her disposal. It means that where you're concerned, there *aren't* any alternatives."

"Why not?"

"You may have your own protection. It might be something you own, a charm or brooch, something you have on you all the time," suggested Waldorf. Ophelia said she didn't have anything like that. "In that case, it might be something in you."

"Like being immune?" asked Ophelia.

"Very like it. But I can't tell how immune you are, or what exactly is protecting you, so I'd hate to take any risks."

"If Mary were successful in getting me to drink something, how would she explain my absence, and Gran's for that matter, to school when it opens again, or the postman, or the milkman?" asked Ophelia.

"They have two choices," Waldorf replied. "Either they tell the few people who are curious enough to ask that your grandmother sold the house to them, or they take your places."

"How?" cried Ophelia.

"They could grow to look like you," said Waldorf. "And nobody would know the difference." Ophelia shuddered.

When Ophelia finally plucked up the courage to go downstairs, she found Mary standing by the sink in the kitchen, and talking animatedly to a strange-looking girl sitting next to the Doctor, who was still asleep in his chair. The conversation stopped when they saw Ophelia. They didn't appear to notice Waldorf sneaking in behind her.

Ophelia stared at the girl curiously. It hadn't been possible to tell what she looked like in the dim light of the bedroom. She was tall and incredibly thin, wearing clothes that could have been an old school uniform meant for someone taller still, all in grey. Ophelia thought she could be about eighteen. The girl's eyes were like tiny green and yellow sparks in her thin, pale face; they were too close together and glared at Ophelia malevolently from beneath a shock of black, shoulder-length hair.

"Gran might have employed you to look after us, Mary," said Ophelia quietly, "but she didn't say you could have guests." She was determined to act as though nothing had happened earlier. Mary never tried to touch her when she was awake, so she would be all right as long as she stayed awake.

"Meet my niece," said Mary in a lazy voice. "And there's not much for your grandmother to complain about, since she's hardly in a fit state to notice that Blackie is even here."

"Heeello," said Blackie in a thin, high-pitched voice like the wrong note on a violin.

Waldorf came up and put his paws on the table to take a closer look at the visitor. Blackie let out an ear-piercing yell and scrambled on to the table. Waldorf kept looking at her, unperturbed by her outburst. For a moment she stared back, her hair standing on end, then, before Ophelia realised what was happening, Blackie leapt over Waldorf's head and shot out of the kitchen door. He chased her through the house, into the garden and up the apple tree outside Grandmother's window.

Ophelia called Waldorf away, leaving Blackie quaking and hissing in the branches. "I want you to get rid of that dog!" shouted Mary, appearing with an umbrella from the hatstand in the hallway, and waving it menacingly.

"I think it's back to the bedroom," grumbled Ophelia, smiling faintly at the sight of an ugly, teenage girl clinging to the limb of an apple tree, spitting like water on a hotplate.

Ophelia shut the bedroom door behind her. "I'm going to have to find a way to put a lock or a bolt on here," she told Waldorf, "otherwise I won't dare go to sleep again."

"You could always put the bed against the door," suggested the dog, "then, even if they do get in again, they are bound to wake you."

"You wouldn't have to," said a deep voice from the corner of the room, "if you'd let me help you." Ophelia drew a sharp breath. There, by the wardrobe, stood a strange man.

Everything he wore was grey. Even his hair was grey. He was so grey, in fact, that he gave the impression of being no more than a fog on the wall. But as he stepped forward his outline grew more distinct. He was very thin and tall, towering over Ophelia. The growl in Waldorf's throat died as the man reached out his hand to shake Ophelia's, and introduced himself as Michael. "I'm here in answer to your advert," he announced.

"Of course!" cried Ophelia with relief. "Oh, I'm so pleased to meet you. I didn't realise the advert would be in the paper so soon. But shouldn't a witch be a woman?"

"I suppose you should call me a warlock," grinned Michael, his face creasing into hundreds of little lines that gathered around his mouth and eyes. Ophelia realised he must be a lot older than he looked.

"I put the advert in the paper because there's a woman downstairs, a witch, who refuses to leave," explained Ophelia. "So I need another witch to get rid of her. How magic are you?"

"Aaaah," said Michael, "now we have the interview! Is there some trick you would like me to do?"

"Not really," said Ophelia, wishing she could think of something all the same. "I'd just like you

51

to make Mary and her familiar go away. But I don't know what I could pay you. I haven't any money."

"Payment isn't necessary," answered Michael, waving a dismissive hand. "Now, I think I'd better get to work. You understand, of course, there is no guarantee that I'll succeed. I can only try." He snapped his fingers and a small flame appeared on the end of his thumb; he blew on it and it travelled up the sleeve of his grey jacket, across his chest and down the other arm. He held it in the palm of his hand for a moment, before tossing it in the air, where it floated gently. Then he snapped his fingers again and the flame disappeared with a popping sound.

"So what happens now?" asked Ophelia, still watching the space where the flame had been.

"I go downstairs and attempt to persuade your unwelcome guests to leave. I suggest you remain here, for safety's sake," he replied. On his way out he stroked the side of the door a few times. There was a fizzing, popping noise and a blister appeared in the paintwork. He tapped it with his forefinger and the paint fell away to reveal a large, heavy-duty bolt. He did the same to the door frame and produced the socket for it.

"You nearly forgot," he said, turning to smile at Ophelia.

Michael had only been gone for a few seconds when the noises began downstairs. Ophelia was itching to go and look, but Waldorf wouldn't hear of it. "But it sounds as though they're throwing the furniture around!" she argued.

"Take that!" she heard Mary screech. This was followed by the howl of a cat that had been trodden on.

"Let that be a lesson to you!" they heard Michael shout.

"It's all sounding quite hopeful," said Ophelia.

Then there was a crash, as though someone had thrown a sideboard at the wall. It made the house shake; books fell off Ophelia's bookcase, and her only two pictures fell off the wall and smashed.

Twenty minutes later, Ophelia's bedroom door swung slowly open and an embarrassed-looking baby elephant walked in.

"Ahem," said the baby elephant. "I have to say that I have always considered myself to be pretty good at what I do, but that housekeeper of yours cheats like blazes. I'm awfully sorry, but I shall have to leave now. It's going to take quite a while to work out an antidote to my trunk." With this, the baby elephant turned in the doorway, and with a flick of his stringy tail, was gone.

"That was Michael," gasped Ophelia.

"I'm afraid so," sighed Waldorf. "Now we'll just have to wait for the next applicant."

"How do you know there'll be one?"

"I don't," he said.

Nothing happened until the post arrived. That, in itself, was quite an event, because post was something the house rarely received. It was even more unusual that Ophelia should receive a parcel, because she didn't know anyone who would send her one.

"Don't just stare at it," said Waldorf excitedly. "Open it!"

Ophelia pulled off the brown wrapping paper to reveal an enormous, deflated, yellow rubber balloon, neatly folded.

"There must be a reason for you getting it," said Waldorf in a puzzled voice. "Isn't there a note?" Ophelia shook her head. "You'd better blow it up then," he advised. "It's what ballons are for. Who knows, the balloon itself might be a message."

The balloon was so big they had to take turns in blowing, and Waldorf climbed out of the top part of his skin in order to be able to do so more easily, slipping back into it the moment he had tied a knot in the mouthpiece.

"Look, it's in the shape of an old woman!" said Ophelia in surprise.

"A very old woman with a handbag," observed Waldorf, studying the bobbing

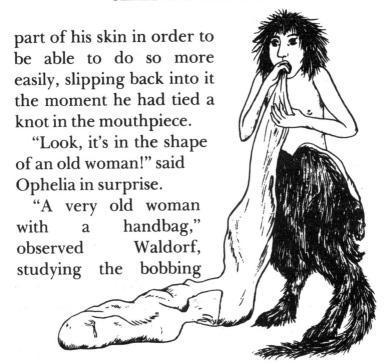

balloon. The balloon came to rest on the floor, rocking slightly, the way balloons do. Then it twitched and the rocking became more violent and more purposeful. A split appeared in the side of the balloon, though it didn't burst. The split grew longer and longer until Waldorf and Ophelia could see that there was a *real* woman inside the balloon.

The woman peeled the rubber from her arms and legs and emerged complete with glasses, like a butterfly from a chrysalis. She was as yellow from head to foot as the balloon had been. She stood up, straightened her skirt, tucked the strap of her handbag more firmly into the crook of her elbow, and peered over her glasses at Ophelia and Waldorf.

"Which one of you is Ophelia?" she asked. Ophelia raised her hand slightly to indicate that she was; she hadn't quite found her voice yet.

"I'm sorry I had to arrive like this," explained the woman, "but my sense of direction is hopeless, so I use the post. I can always be sure to reach the correct address by post. My name, by the way, is Miss Walton, and I've just seen your advert." Like Michael, she shook hands with Ophelia.

Ophelia didn't ask how Miss Walton could see the advert *and* get herself through the postal system all in one morning. Instead, she told Miss Walton why they needed help. She was honest enough to mention that Michael had failed in his efforts.

"I, too, can only do my best," said Miss Walton, "but I'd like to try and help."

"May I watch this time?" asked Ophelia. Waldorf caught her eye and she realised he disapproved.

"I suppose if you've gone this long without coming to any harm, there's no reason why you shouldn't," replied Miss Walton, "though I must say it's odd you haven't been dealt with already."

"She has tried to put me to sleep," admitted Ophelia. "With some soup."

"There, you see what I mean?" cried Miss Walton. "If she couldn't get you to eat the soup, she could have turned you into some small, insignificant rodent, and given you to a stupid little boy who forgot to feed you more than once a week. She could have turned you into a pineapple and chopped you into a fruit salad; she could have done almost anything, but she hasn't. I'd say that, for some strange reason, you're safe. Unless she's saving you up for something special, though that's unlikely if she's already tried to put you to sleep. Are you going to introduce me to her?"

Ophelia cleared her throat nervously. "Can I ask you one favour, just in case, um, well, it doesn't work out, though I'm sure it will. Would it be possible for you to open the door to Gran's bedroom? I'm sure she hasn't been awake at all since yesterday morning and I want to see how she is."

"My pleasure. Just lead the way," replied Miss Walton.

Ophelia half expected Grandmother's door to have vanished again, but Mary wasn't aware of Miss Walton's presence and wasn't taking precautions.

Confronted with the locked door, Miss Walton slung her bright yellow handbag further back on her arm and rubbed her yellow hands together. Then she stroked the nail of her right forefinger; she stroked and stroked, and the more she stroked the longer the nail became.

Then she rubbed her left thumb and forefinger up and down the sides of it, making it narrower. When this was done to her apparent satisfaction, the nail was about four inches long and as thin as a skewer. She slipped it into the keyhole and carefully twisted it first one way, then the other. There was a click; she turned the door handle and the door swung open. Ophelia breathed a sigh of relief and stepped into the room.

"That's a handy trick you have there," said Waldorf before he could stop himself.

"Aaaah, I thought you talked," smiled Miss Walton. "I wondered why you were being so quiet."

"Force of habit in company," grinned Waldorf.

"As for the trick," said Miss Walton, "a hairpin would have done as well, but if I used one of mine it would ruin my bun, and it took me ages to do this morning."

"Gran," Ophelia was whispering. "Gran, it's me, wake up; we have to get you out of here."

She was standing by the bed, her face pale and stricken. Grandmother lay there so quietly it was difficult to know whether there was still life in her body. The whole room, including Grandmother, was covered in a thickening film of white dust.

Ophelia reached down and took her grandmother's hand. It was so cold that she found herself putting her fingers on the old lady's pulse the way she had seen the Doctor do. With a shudder, she noticed that not only were the veins in the wrist becoming plainly visible beneath the skin, but so were the bones: she could actually see her grandmother's knuckles.

"Gran, please wake up," she pleaded more urgently. She tugged at the old lady's arm, but her grandmother was as limp as a wet flannel. Miss Walton came over to have a closer look.

"You can't move her, dear," she said sympathetically. "I'd know those signs anywhere: she's had a long-term course of sleeping soup if ever I saw it. She'll eventually disappear if she continues to take it. Look, she's vanishing already. I'd give her three weeks at the most – judging by her appearance – before she vanishes altogether."

"But the Doctor has had some too," protested Ophelia. "Will he disappear as well?" She was too stunned to cry, and if she began to cry now, she would never stop.

"The Doctor won't disappear unless he's being given the soup on a regular basis. One dose will just put you to sleep for a few days, two doses will last much longer, three doses and you'll begin to fade slightly. A dozen doses and you'll sleep for weeks, growing fainter by the day. There is always a full recovery on waking, however, though if the soup continues to be administered the victim will fade completely, before they are able to be woken. Does that explain it?" asked Miss Walton.

Ophelia nodded heavily.

"Gran's had more than a dozen doses," she said almost inaudibly. "Couldn't we just carry her out of here, and take her somewhere where she has a chance to wake up?"

Miss Walton shook her head. "She's too far gone to wake naturally before she vanishes. She can only be cured if she stays where she is and the person who caused the sleep is removed. It doesn't work the other way around. Once Mary is gone, an antidote spell can be applied and expected to work. It won't work while Mary is still in the building."

Mary and Blackie were in the kitchen, surrounded by every saucepan and bowl in the house. "Here, try this one," said Mary, taking a pot from the hob and feeding Blackie a spoonful of its contents. Ophelia gasped. In the past hour, Mary's short, tatty locks had grown as long and grey as her grandmother's, and Blackie was squeezed into one of Ophelia's old summer dresses, and her black hair was turning as brown as Ophelia's own.

"I've come to ask you to leave," announced Miss Walton, just as Mary was putting the pan back on the stove.

"I shall ignore that request and ask you to leave yourself," retorted Mary. "I'm sure Ophelia told you what happened to the last person who attempted to get rid of us. This is my home now, and that makes me stronger."

Miss Walton began to mutter something under her breath. Mary listened for a moment to words which Ophelia couldn't understand at all, then flew into a rage.

"How dare you use that on me! I'm not a ghost you can exorcise!" She put her hand in the pan on the cooker, and scooping out a thick glob of brown syrup, she threw it at Miss Walton, who vanished in the nick of time, so that the sludge hit the wall instead. Miss Walton reappeared on the other side of the room, just behind the sleeping Doctor. The next handful hit the Doctor on the shoulder and began to run down his arm.

Miss Walton opened her handbag and slid her arm into it right up to the elbow. Her hand emerged holding a gold bird cage that appeared too big to fit into such a small bag. She placed the cage on the table, then pulled out a second one and put it beside the first.

"They're a bit small for us, don't you think?" Mary sneered. Blackie grinned, revealing small, white, pointed teeth.

"Oh, I think you'll fit into these," said Miss Walton confidently. She fixed Mary with her eye and began to mutter under her breath. Mary grabbed Blackie and hid behind her. Miss Walton stared into Blackie's face and kept muttering.

"What's happening to me?" wailed Blackie, forced to hold Miss Walton's gaze.

Ophelia crouched with Waldorf in the corner by the kitchen door, watching the proceedings with growing apprehension, but determined not to be frightened off: after all, this was something she would never see again.

"What's Miss Walton saying?" she whispered to Waldorf. He shook his head to show he had no idea.

Blackie began to whimper. "Hey, what are you doing to her?" demanded Mary. Miss Walton kept on muttering.

Blackie was shrinking, and the more Miss Walton muttered, the smaller Blackie became. Mary kept pulling her upwards by the arms as though that would stretch her. Then she, too, began to whisper under her breath, and the more Mary whispered, the bigger Blackie grew. Miss Walton's voice got louder – though the words were no less incomprehensible – and Blackie got smaller again.

It wasn't long before both Mary and Miss Walton were sitting on the floor exhausted, their throats sore and their voices hoarse. Blackie, who had previously been considerably taller than Ophelia, now only came up to her shoulder.

"I'm not staying like this," protested Blackie in a high-pitched squeak. She stepped over the prostrate forms of Mary and Miss Walton and stomped over to the cooker on tiny feet. With one sweep of her tiny arm, she cleared it of pots and pans. Then she searched the cupboard beneath the sink until she came up with one small pan, and began throwing in bits and pieces from a selection of odd weeds on the table.

"A little bit of this and a little piece of that," she was saying to herself. She added water to her concoction, allowed it to simmer for a minute, and drank it.

Slowly, she began to swell and grow.

"She's fatter than she used to be," whispered Ophelia. Blackie certainly was fatter, and Ophelia's dress looked as though it was on the point of splitting.

"I think we should wait outside," Waldorf hissed. "It's going to get very untidy in here, and I would feel a lot happier if you weren't in the firing line."

Mary and Miss Walton had climbed to their feet again and were now muttering strange language at each other. Every so often Miss Walton reached into her bag again and threw something at Mary – powder, or grains of sand, or liquid from a bottle – and Mary reciprocated by muttering over a plant or an insect she'd picked up from the table and throwing it at Miss Walton.

"I can't believe any of this is going to work," said Ophelia quietly as she and Waldorf edged round the kitchen door.

They sat on the stairs in the hall, listening to the voices getting louder and louder until they were shouting. Then suddenly, it all stopped.

Ophelia held her breath and waited.

The kitchen door swung open. For a moment, Ophelia thought there was nothing there, then her gaze dropped to the floor. Waddling towards them was Miss Walton, squashed into one of her own cages with her feet, still clad in their bright yellow shoes, sticking through the bars.

The apparition tilted violently from side to side, finding it difficult to walk itself under the circumstances. "I'm awfully sorry," came Miss Walton's muffled voice from the mass of yellow clothing, "but two against one is too many. Could you open the front door for me, please?"

Ophelia obliged, and watched the cage on the two yellow feet totter down the garden path to the open gate.

"That's it," sighed Ophelia. "There surely can't be anyone else to come."

"Nonsense," said Waldorf brightly. "The day isn't over yet; it's only just lunchtime."

"Talking about lunch, isn't that Mrs Wolf coming up the street with a casserole in her hands?" said Ophelia suddenly, craning her neck to see over the hedge.

"I wouldn't know," replied Waldorf. "I've never seen her."

"It *is* Mrs Wolf," cried Ophelia. "What do we do now?"

"We tell her anything to get rid of her and keep the casserole," advised Waldorf dryly.

Mrs Wolf turned into the garden and walked up to the front door. "Hello, Ophelia dear," she said pleasantly. "I hope your grandmother won't mind, but I've brought her a chicken casserole." She held up the earthenware dish she was carrying wrapped in a blue-checked tea towel. "It's still quite hot, though I'm sure your housekeeper could put it in the oven for a few minutes."

"Please let me take it in for you," said Ophelia quickly as Mrs Wolf tried to get past her.

"It's no trouble for me just to take it into the kitchen," smiled Mrs Wolf, "and it would give me a chance to meet your new housekeeper, and ask my husband if he needs anything else."

"Please, Mrs Wolf," begged Ophelia, "don't come in. Gran is so ill and Doctor Wolf has been at her bedside constantly. He refuses to be disturbed; he won't even let me in. If you leave the casserole with me, I'll make sure Mary warms it up later when the Doctor takes a break. I know he and Gran will really appreciate the thought."

"Oh, very well," sighed Mrs Wolf in a quivering voice. "I'll come back and collect the dish tonight."

She was gone before Ophelia could say she would return it herself.

"Well done," Waldorf congratulated her. "We get to eat today!"

"But Mrs Wolf will be back again later," Ophelia reminded him, "and we'll have to get rid of her all over again, or she'll end up like Gran and the Doctor."

They sat disconsolately in Ophelia's bedroom and shared the casserole between them.

Chapter Three

By three o'clock in the afternoon, Ophelia had given up all hope of another white witch arriving. And even if one did, she doubted they would be able to get rid of Mary and Blackie.

"We're going to have at least one more applicant for the job," said Waldorf suddenly.

"How do you know?" asked Ophelia in surprise.

"I can hear faint footsteps on the path," he replied. "This one is actually going to call at the door for a change."

"Quick, we must get downstairs before Mary answers it!" cried Ophelia.

She needn't have worried: Mary and Blackie were laughing and talking loudly in the kitchen, too engrossed to bother about anything else.

"Hello," said the woman on the doorstep a trifle tersely. She was about Mary's age and almost as fat as Mary had been before she had begun to lose weight in her efforts to look like Gran. She was dressed in an orange skirt, a green shirt and yellow wellingtons, and looked dreadful.

"I've come in answer to the advert," said the woman sharply. Ophelia liked her rather less than she had liked Michael and Miss Walton. "Can I speak to the person who placed the advert?" she said.

"That was me," confessed Ophelia.

"Can't have been you," said the woman. "You're only a child." She peered over Ophelia's head expectantly.

"Are you a white witch?" asked Ophelia.

"More of a grey one," replied the woman, "but I can still do any job a namby-pamby white witch can do; I just have more understanding of what the not-so-white witches are capable of. So you really put the advert in?" Ophelia assured her she had. "Well, are you going to keep me standing on the doorstep all day?" demanded the woman. Reluctantly, Ophelia showed her into the living room.

"My name is Veronica," said the newcomer, looking round the room with disdain. The walls were covered in paintings and plates that Ophelia's grandmother had spent years collecting, and the shelves were adorned with intricate little ornaments.

"I'm Ophelia," said Ophelia, holding out her hand.

Veronica ignored it. "So what's the job and how much does it pay?" she wanted to know.

Ophelia gaped. Waldorf looked up at her and shook his head. He didn't seem to think this was right either.

"I thought white witches worked for nothing," said Ophelia lamely. "The other two did ... Besides, I don't have any money until Gran wakes up."

"Well, the other two witches were no good, were they, or you wouldn't be needing me. You would have turned me away on the doorstep. As for white witches working for nothing, I've already told you, I'm a grey witch. How long is your grandmother going to be asleep?" She was examining a Victorian plate with what looked to Ophelia like a practised eye.

"Until you get rid of the witch in the kitchen, and wake her up," Ophelia told her. "Oh, and there's the Doctor as well; he's asleep too."

Veronica raised her eyebrows. "Sounds like you most certainly do need my help," she commented with a half-smile. "I'll just have to see what you've got around the house that might do as payment for my services."

"Do you think she's more likely to succeed than the others because she's not as 'good' as they were?" Ophelia whispered to Waldorf.

"No idea," he told her under his breath. "But I think we've reached the stage where we'll try anything, don't you?"

Ophelia agreed.

"There are some rather nice pieces in here that might do," said Veronica in a condescending tone. "Now, why don't you show me where the problem is?"

"At least she's businesslike," whispered Waldorf as Ophelia led Veronica to the kitchen. She hesitated outside for a moment, to see what she could hear.

"Sssssh, be quiet," she heard Mary whisper. "I think the brat's brought someone else in. This should be amusing." Blackie replied with a high-pitched violin note.

Ophelia swung the door open. "I've brought another visitor," she announced, with far more courage than she felt. If Veronica frightens *me*, she thought to herself, she must surely be a little more daunting to Mary than the other two witches were.

There was a long silence as Mary and Veronica stared at each other. "Veronica," said Mary at last. Ophelia looked at Veronica in horror: Mary knew her!

Veronica dropped the carpet bag she had been carrying and opened her arms. "Mary Cage!" she cried in delight. "I barely recognised you, you look so slim and your hair is so long and grey!" It was true, Mary was so like Grandmother now, she was almost unrecognisable as herself. The two women greeted each other enthusiastically.

"I'm having a change of appearance to suit my new home," laughed Mary.

Ophelia looked over at Blackie and felt the floor heave beneath her feet; it was like looking at her own reflection, though Blackie was still tall, and her eyes still glittered like green and yellow sparks.

"The potion works gradually," Mary was explaining to Veronica. "Because we need time to get used to our new faces. It would be a bit of a shock for me to grow old in a moment; Ophelia's grandmother must be years older than me."

"Oh no," wailed Ophelia.

"Where have you been all these years?" Mary asked Veronica. "I haven't seen you since we became housekeepers to that minister in the big

house, and *you* took on *his* appearance."

Veronica shook with laughter and said she'd grown to look like a lot of people in her time, but never a man and never a minister, until then.

"We didn't put him to sleep though, did we?" giggled Mary. "We locked him in the broom cupboard without a voice to cry for help with, and fed him on scraps!"

"And he was there for years!" howled Veronica. "Long after you decided you wanted to move on. You should have heard the sermons I gave in his place! I stayed there until just recently, when one of the walls of the building collapsed."

"Was it the bit with the broom cupboard in it?" squealed Mary and the two women collapsed on each other's shoulders in fits of laughter.

Quietly, Ophelia and Waldorf slipped out of the room.

"This is too much!" said Ophelia, tears running down her cheeks. "Our problem has just doubled. Veronica isn't going to help now; she's going to move in! And did you see how much Mary looked like Gran? They even have the same noses. And Blackie looks just like me!"

"She still smells like a cat," grunted Waldorf. "Ophelia, neither of us could have known about Veronica. You can't blame yourself."

"Oh, I'm not blaming myself, or you," moaned Ophelia. "I just feel so helpless." Then she wiped her eyes. "There is one thing we haven't done yet though," she said. "We haven't searched Mary's room. Now she's so busy with Veronica, we've got a chance to."

Waldorf didn't like the idea, even though he thought it was a good one in principle.

The foul smell in the room hit them as soon as they opened the door and almost made Ophelia turn away. But she swallowed her revulsion and went in, trying not to breathe too deeply.

The patterned carpet was covered in grit and muddy footprints from Mary's weed-collecting excursions; the bed was a tangle of sheets and blankets; but, other than the few pieces of furniture and Mary's carpet bag, the room appeared to be empty.

Ophelia went to the wardrobe first and opened it. There were no clothes or shoes, but the stench was stronger here. It emanated from the bottom of the wardrobe, where a pile of strange plants lay heaped and tangled, oozing foul liquid as they decayed. The head of one of the plants raised itself like the head of a dying animal, and let out a desperate gurgle, before falling back into the morass. Quickly, Ophelia shut the door again.

"Some housekeeper!" said Waldorf.

Next, Ophelia tried the dressing table, but all the drawers were empty. On top were a few nut-like objects, seeds from some strange and enormous plant, and a bowl of dried insects. "Midnight snack," said Waldorf.

There was nothing under the bed but balls of dust. Which only left the bag on the chair ...

"If there's nothing in here, we're stuck, and I think we're going to be stuck," Ophelia sighed. One by one she began taking out the contents of the carpet bag and laying them on the floor.

First there was a selection of tiny bottles and jars with labels whose writing was so faded it was illegible. Then there were more dried seed pods and a small black notebook. Ophelia tried to read what was written in the notebook, but the words looked foreign. "I think it's a different language," she told Waldorf.

"It'll be Mary's language," he said. "Each witch has her own kind of shorthand."

Ophelia stuffed the little book into the breast pocket of her shirt. Part of her hated to touch it because of who it belonged to, but part of her was delighted at being able to steal something from someone so evil. She felt as though she had made a small strike back at Mary.

"What are you going to do with it?" Waldorf asked curiously.

"If we find someone else who wants to help us," said Ophelia, "they might be able to translate it."

"You're learning fast," grinned Waldorf.

There was nothing else in the bag but a pile of those grotty bits of fluff and unidentifiable gritty bits that gather at the bottom of handbags when they are never cleaned out. Ophelia put everything back the way she had found it.

"Now," she said, "there is one other thing we should do ..." Waldorf cocked his head at her. "We should get the Doctor out of the kitchen. It's bad enough that he's been in there all this time with Mary and Blackie, but with Veronica there as well, there's no telling what they might get up to. They might use him to experiment on, or something."

"At least he doesn't have to remain in the house," said Waldorf. "The dose of sleeping soup that he's had will wear off eventually, and I'm fairly certain they haven't bothered to give him any more of it."

"He's too heavy for us to take him very far," Ophelia pointed out, "but we could at least drag him into the living room."

Ophelia was terrified at the prospect of going back into the kitchen. "Don't worry," whispered Waldorf, "I can get rid of at least one of them."

He was as good as his word: as soon as they were through the door, he flew at Blackie, who was in the process of sharpening her long fingernails on the walls. She screamed and threw herself out of the open window. Ophelia caught sight of her running down the street on all fours.

"Can't you do something about the girl?" asked Veronica in exasperation, nodding her head in Ophelia's direction.

Mary deposited another pan on the heap that now rose from the sink. She whispered something in Veronica's ear that made them both roar with laughter. There was a look of pure delight on Mary's copy of Grandmother's face.

"I see," said Veronica. Then she smiled at

Ophelia. "You really do have something to look forward to," she said.

Ophelia avoided her eyes and busied herself with the Doctor. She wedged both hands under one of the sleeping man's armpits, and Waldorf sank his teeth into the Doctor's other sleeve. Together they began to pull and tug at him in an attempt to dislodge him from his chair. But he was so big and heavy he was almost impossible to move.

"What do you suppose they're trying to do?" Mary asked Veronica in amusement.

"I think they're trying to take him away," replied Veronica, with a stupid smile on her face.

Mary grabbed a saucepan from the table, dipped her hand into it and scooped out a thick black solution. Working quickly, she daubed the Doctor with it. Ophelia and Waldorf stepped away to avoid the muck.

"What are you doing?" Ophelia cried.

Mary didn't answer, nor did she take any notice of Waldorf, who was growling and snarling and tearing at her skirt.

Mary stood back to admire her handiwork. She spoke a peculiar word as she did so. Ophelia reached out to take hold of the Doctor again, but Waldorf caught her wrist gently in his mouth, and stopped her.

Before their very eyes, the Doctor began to change. His clothes seemed to melt and dissolve and his face and hands began to twitch and quiver. Bit by bit he became green all over; his clothes and skin blended together and sprouted scales. As soon as the change was complete, the green skin erupted in purple spots.

"Very nice, Mary my dear," smiled Veronica, "but it needs a little something else ..." The two women stood shoulder to shoulder surveying the bright green dragon with purple spots.

"I know!" exclaimed Veronica. She shut her eyes for a moment, muttered a few words and snapped her fingers. The dragon's short, spiky ears grew and ballooned.

"What are they?" asked Mary with interest.

"Mouse ears," replied Veronica. "Adds an individual touch, don't you think?"

They were interrupted by a banging on the front door. Ophelia hesitated.

"You go, brat," said Mary. "It's probably someone *else* coming to see if they can get rid of us. Just send them in. We'll send them out again when we've finished with them." She gave a coarse laugh and wiped a drip off the end of her nose with the sleeve of her satin shirt.

Ophelia and Waldorf went to the door, only to find Mrs Wolf standing there. "Oh no!" whispered Ophelia to Waldorf. "I'd forgotten all about her."

'Hello, Mrs Wolf," said Ophelia uncertainly. "I suppose you've come for the casserole dish."

"Not this time," said Mrs Wolf with a strange smile. "I've come for the interview." Ophelia noticed her fingers weren't twitching the way they normally did.

"I don't know what you're talking about," protested Ophelia. "There are no interviews here."

"Ophelia dear, I realise this may come as a bit of a surprise, but like most people I do read the local paper. I saw your advert and, unlike some, I knew it wasn't a joke."

"But only a real witch would take it seriously," blurted Ophelia before she could stop herself.

"That's right," said Mrs Wolf with a smile.

"No, no, you can't be, not really. You're not, are you?" stuttered Ophelia.

"Not what?" asked Mrs Wolf innocently. Suddenly, she seemed a totally different character.

"A witch," said Ophelia.

"I most certainly am," said Mrs Wolf. She

looked as though she was enjoying Ophelia's discomfort. "I'm not a brilliant witch, but I get by, and even if I can't cure your problem, I can most certainly help. Do you want to interview me?"

Before Ophelia could answer, Mrs Wolf pushed past her and strode into the living room. Ophelia and Waldorf watched from the doorway as she placed herself neatly in the centre of the room.

"For an interview," said Mrs Wolf, "one needs the correct attire." She shut her eyes and began to hum softly, hugging herself and swaying gently from side to side. As she moved, her drab clothes and flowered apron began to twist and blur, weaving themselves into a pink blouse, a pink skirt and pink shoes.

Mrs Wolf peered at the results of her efforts in the mirror above the mantlepiece. "There's something missing," she muttered. She swept her hand over her straggling curls and they became a French twist, and wiped her face with her fingers to reveal lipstick, blusher and eye shadow.

"Now," she said, turning to Ophelia, "will I do?"

Ophelia nodded dumbly.

"I think you had better explain the problem

we're having with Mary," said Waldorf quietly and Mrs Wolf threw him an approving glance.

"But we've had two other white witches already," Ophelia reminded him, "and they both failed dismally."

"Aah, I might not be a wonderful witch," answered Mrs Wolf, "but I have unusually strong protection. So it's Mary who is the trouble, then?"

"And Blackie and Veronica," added Waldorf.

Mrs Wolf raised her eyebrows. "Where is Doctor Wolf in all this?" she enquired. Ophelia found she couldn't look Mrs Wolf in the eye. "I only want to help you," said Mrs Wolf gently. "I'm not really the mousey little woman you think I am."

Ophelia nearly burst into tears at the kindness in her voice. "Why did you pretend you were?" she asked.

"Because I wanted to help the Doctor by being more like the wife his patients expected. And he would think I was crazy if I told him I was a witch. If I went so far as to prove it, he would think *he* was crazy."

"Everyone is in the kitchen," said Ophelia, "except for Gran, who is asleep upstairs and won't wake up."

Mrs Wolf strode into the kitchen like a ship in full sail.

"Oh no, how tedious, it *is* another one! You were right, Mary," sighed Veronica.

"It's a real pain in the neck," complained Mary, ignoring Mrs Wolf and Ophelia. "I suppose we shall just have to dispose of her like the others." She tossed her long grey hair impatiently over her shoulder.

"This must be the Doctor," said Mrs Wolf briskly, going up to the dragon and tweaking one of his mouse ears. Ophelia nodded. "Well, it would be better if we got him out of the way. We can park him in the garden."

With astonishing strength, Mrs Wolf took hold of her husband by his tail, put it over her shoulder and dragged him out into the back garden. As she passed them, both Mary and Veronica chanted runes and spells, but whatever they were saying had no effect. They looked at each other in surprise.

Ophelia stared: Mrs Wolf's entire body was encompassed in the blue light. She and Waldorf followed her into the garden. "Why are you blue?" asked Ophelia curiously.

"That's the protection I was telling you about. I call it the 'blue bubble' effect," answered Mrs Wolf, propping the Doctor

against the trunk of the apple tree.

"What's that?" Ophelia wanted to know.

"It's when you imagine yourself to be surrounded by a blue glow, and magic can't hurt you," Mrs Wolf told Ophelia. "It doesn't have to be visible to protect you, but the stronger it is, the more it shows."

Ophelia hugged herself. It was getting colder. "Waldorf thinks I might have my own protection," she said self-consciously. "I think he might be right because Mary hasn't used her magic on me."

Mrs Wolf studied Ophelia carefully for a moment. "It's possible," she said finally. "Were your parents witches?"

"Not that I know of," replied Ophelia. "In fact, I'm certain they weren't. They were killed in an accident when I was little."

"Oh dear, oh I am sorry," muttered Mrs Wolf. "Well, they wouldn't be witches then, not if they were, well, in an accident they couldn't get out of. Perhaps you're a natural?"

"What's that?" asked Ophelia.

"Witches tend to be the children of witches," Mrs Wolf explained. "It's like a family business, though the skill still has to be learned. However, sometimes there's a quirk, and a child is born with natural ability and, therefore, natural protection, both of which can easily be improved. It doesn't seem to matter if the parents are witches or not, but it's very rare. Would you like to find out if you are a natural?"

Ophelia shrugged her shoulders. "If you think I should," she said. She was actually longing to know.

"I want you to stand quite still while I throw a small thunderbolt at you," said Mrs Wolf, positioning Ophelia away from the apple tree on an open piece of lawn.

"What?" asked Ophelia, not quite believing her ears.

"Oh, it won't hurt at all," promised Mrs Wolf. "At worst, it might singe your eyebrows a bit; other than that, it's perfectly safe. Trust me. Just imagine you're surrounded by blue light."

Waldorf stood aside. "Don't worry, Ophelia," he said smiling. "I'm sure she knows what she's doing."

"I wish I knew what *I* was doing," replied Ophelia. But she thought hard about being blue.

Mrs Wolf seemed to be concentrating. Suddenly, she flicked her fingers towards Ophelia, and released a tiny bolt of lightning that snaked through the air in the gathering dusk. It hit Ophelia full in the chest and fizzled out. She didn't feel a thing.

"You're right, Mrs Wolf!" she cried. "It didn't hurt at all!"

"This is where I have to confess it would have knocked you over if you didn't have some kind of self-defence," Mrs Wolf admitted. "But I was positive you did, or Mary wouldn't have allowed you to remain untouched. Now, you're going to let me try again."

"I am?" questioned Ophelia. But before she had time to argue, Mrs Wolf sent a larger bolt of lightning streaking towards her. This one illuminated the whole garden and spat and crackled as it zigzagged across the lawn and hit Ophelia as the first had done. There was a shower of sparks as it bounced off her and disappeared into the grass with a hissing noise and a cloud of steam from evaporating dew.

"I was right!" cried Mrs Wolf triumphantly. "I was right. You have the most tremendous reflective powers!"

"So what does that mean?" Ophelia enquired.

"It means," said Waldorf in a satisfied tone, "that you are a natural witch, and explains why I have been able to talk since I've been with you. It had nothing at all to do with the fact that Mary lives in the same house."

"He's right," agreed Mrs Wolf. "Oh, if I had natural talent as strong as yours I could do anything! Mind you, I would still have to take lessons to improve and control it."

"Could Ophelia do that?" asked Waldorf.

"Absolutely," replied Mrs Wolf. "In fact, we could try and enroll her in my old school – it's run by a friend of mine, Miss Rose. Then we would be in a better position to rid Ophelia's grandmother of her unwelcome visitors. You see, on my own, I simply don't have the strength or the knowledge."

"But what would happen to Gran and Waldorf if I went to this school?" protested Ophelia. "It would take ages to teach me anything, assuming I could be taught at all. How could I help Gran if I was away at school?"

Mrs Wolf pointed out that even two weeks of tuition would make a great improvement. "Every little helps," she told Ophelia. "And who knows? You might be a quick learner. Two weeks and maybe a few days and you could still be back in time to help her, only by then you would have some idea of the extent of your abilities."

"If it takes that long," groaned Ophelia, "Gran will be as transparent as a jellyfish by the time I get back."

"Put it this way, Ophelia," said Mrs Wolf, "if you don't go, your grandmother will vanish anyway, and there will be nothing I or anyone else can do to prevent it. Waldorf will go to school with you as your familiar, because all witches must have one. No doubt Veronica's will turn up soon enough."

"I'll stay here and keep an eye on your grandmother, and make sure they don't do anything else to my husband. They can't hurt me, though, unfortunately, without help, I can't hurt them either."

"Mrs Wolf is making good sense," said Waldorf.

"I just wish I could learn things at home," sighed Ophelia. "Besides, I'm not sure I'll be any good at a new school. I don't exactly fit into my old one. They all think I'm a bit odd, and I have no idea why."

"Probably your aura," commented Mrs Wolf. "The other children might not know what it is about you that sets you apart, but they would feel it."

"Oh, I get on with them all right," said Ophelia wearily. "But I don't have any particular friends."

"I think you'll find you have a lot more in common with the children you'll meet at the school I'm going to take you to," smiled Mrs Wolf. "But first, we don't want Mary to know you've gone anywhere. Would you like to take me to your room and show me your toys?"

Ophelia was puzzled, but she did as she was asked.

Mrs Wolf chose a large doll that Ophelia had always hated, and a tiny toy horse. She put them on the bed and spoke some words over them. Before Ophelia's eyes the doll and the horse swelled and grew, and as they did so, they took on the features of Waldorf and Ophelia.

"The dolls will take your places. That way Mary won't know you aren't really here," Mrs Wolf grinned. "I can make them move, though sadly I can't make them talk." The Ophelia doll raised a hand and smiled inanely. Her hand fell back into her lap with a dull thud.

Chapter Four

Using the Doctor's car, Mrs Wolf drove them deep into the countryside. By now it was nearly midnight, and it was pitch black except for the headlights. She halted the car in what seemed like the middle of nowhere.

"We can't stop here," protested Ophelia. "There isn't a house for miles!"

"Don't dawdle," said Mrs Wolf briskly. "We have a bit of a walk ahead of us."

"Just put your hand on my shoulder," said Waldorf quietly. "I'll stop you from stumbling; my eyes are better in the dark than yours."

With her fingers twisted in the fur at Waldorf's neck, Ophelia followed Mrs Wolf into the trees that grew at the side of the road. It was so dark she couldn't see the white of her hand in front of her face. Then the trees ended and they found themselves at the edge of a field of tall grass. Ophelia's heart sank; there was still no sign of a building of any kind.

"It's just over here," said Mrs Wolf, taking Ophelia by the hand.

Then she saw it – a tiny red brick building almost hidden by trees on the far side of the field. As they got closer, Ophelia could see that the building had a window in each side of it, through which shone a dull glow. In the narrow wall facing them was a wooden door. It was like a doll's house.

"Is this it?" gasped Ophelia. "It's so small!"

"It's an old telephone exchange," explained Mrs Wolf. "They don't use them any more. Now it's all electronic and dealt with in huge town buildings."

She opened the door to reveal a small concrete interior lit by a large candle on a table in the corner. In the narrow back wall was another door. She pushed it open and led Ophelia and Waldorf through into a long hallway, its ceiling hung at regular intervals with dim lamps.

Just inside the doorway was another little table, this one highly polished, with a hand bell on it.

"Ring the bell," instructed Mrs Wolf.

Ophelia did so, and almost immediately a small figure appeared at the far end of the hallway.

Ophelia watched the approaching figure with a lump in her throat. As it drew closer, she saw that it was a very tall girl with waist-length black hair, wearing an ankle-length black dress.

"Will I have to dress like that?" Ophelia whispered to Mrs Wolf. "That dress is almost see-through."

"I've packed something for you in here," replied Mrs Wolf. She lifted up a small

93

weekend case that Ophelia hadn't noticed in the dark.

At last, the girl reached them. "Miss Rose is expecting you," she said in a cool, clear voice. "Please follow me."

They followed the girl all the way back down the hall, and with every step Ophelia grew more nervous. This was like her first day at school at the age of five – all over again.

After passing several oak doors and empty corridors that led off either side of the hall, they stopped right at the end, in front of an enormous pair of double doors. The tall girl swung open one of the doors and stood aside to allow them to pass through.

They found themselves in a high-ceilinged room hung with crimson velvet curtains. Old, highly polished furniture glowed orange in the light from the fire that burned in the enormous carved stone fireplace. Every surface in the room held a vase of roses, and the air was thick with their scent.

"How could all this have been inside that tiny telephone exchange?" Ophelia whispered to Waldorf.

"We've been walking downhill ever since we came through the door at the other end of the hallway," murmured Waldorf under his breath and Ophelia realised that all the rooms must be underground. There couldn't be any windows behind those velvet curtains.

A woman rose from the elaborately carved desk at the far side of the room. She was wearing a rose-patterned dress with a crimson rose pinned to its large collar, and her long hair was pinned to her head like a cottage loaf.

"Hello," she said. "I see Susannah found you."

The girl glanced at Ophelia and smiled, and her whole face suddenly lit up. Ophelia smiled back.

"Rose," cried Mrs Wolf affectionately. "It's good to see you again." The two women hugged each other. Miss Rose only came up to Mrs Wolf's shoulder.

"I knew you would be coming tonight," smiled Miss Rose. "I get an itch in my right hand if a friend is going to call, and an itch in my left if it's someone less welcome."

Mrs Wolf pushed Ophelia forward. "I've come to see you in the hope that you can help Ophelia," she said. "She's the real reason why I'm here." Briefly she told Miss Rose Ophelia's story.

Miss Rose threw back her head to take a

better look at Ophelia and drew a deep breath.

"Ah, yes, a natural," she sighed happily. "I should have seen it myself." She walked around Ophelia twice. "I don't suppose we shall have you for very long."

"You mean you'll take me?" Ophelia asked.

"Oh yes," replied Miss Rose. "Apart from the fact that we might indeed be able to help you, a 'natural' is just the kind of pupil we like to have. A witch child has quite an advantage over ordinary children when learning the art, because she's brought up with magic all around her, but a natural, even if she's from a normal family, has even greater potential than a witch child."

"Could I learn magic if I was ordinary?" asked Ophelia curiously.

"Oh yes, but you would never be very good at it," replied Miss Rose with satisfaction, "if your parents hadn't brought you up to it. Lessons begin in the cradle, my dear. It's not a job; it's a way of life."

"I'll take Ophelia to the dormitory," said Susannah. "All the others are already in bed."

Ophelia found herself hugging Mrs Wolf goodbye. Then she and Waldorf followed Susannah out of the room. There was a rustling noise in a passage leading off the main corridor, and an intake of breath, then the soft patter of running feet. The sounds were so faint that Ophelia barely heard them. But Waldorf did: he sniffed the air and his ears stood on end, straining to hear.

On the way to the dormitory, Susannah suggested that Ophelia keep the story about her grandmother a secret. "One or two of the other girls will think you're trying to make yourself important, if you talk about it, and might make things difficult for you."

Ophelia thought this was good advice.

Susannah led them to a room with six beds in it, four of which were occupied though none of the occupants was asleep.

"Why did Miss Rose want you?" asked a voice from the corner.

"Because we have a new arrival," answered Susannah. "She's come to stay for a while. Everyone, I'd like you to meet Ophelia."

Now the girls were sitting up in bed. Ophelia noticed that one of the occupied beds had the blankets thrown back at the top, but there seemed to be no one in it.

At the sound of voices, six or seven more girls appeared from the dormitory next door, wanting to know what was happening.

"Your bed's over there," said Susannah,

pointing Ophelia in the direction of a vacant one.

Ophelia went over and put her case on top of it.

One of the girls got out of bed and came over. She was extremely pretty, with blond curls framing a round face, and pouting lips. She was wearing a fancy gypsy-style dress.

"Why aren't you in a nightdress?" scolded Susannah. "You should have got changed long ago."

The girl took no notice. "Is this supposed to be one of us?" she demanded rudely. "She doesn't even look like one of us."

"Since we all look different," said Susannah dryly, "I don't see how you came to that conclusion, so leave her alone and get some sleep." But now the other girls had crowded closer, all eager to have a look at the newcomer.

"This, by the way," said Susannah, pointing to the rude girl, "is Beatrice."

"Look!" cried Beatrice, "she hasn't even got a proper familiar! She's got a dog instead of a cat. Everyone knows that dogs become boys and we can't have a boy in here!"

"A familiar can only become human if its mistress is a practising witch," snapped Susannah, "and since none of us is at that stage,

98

and Ophelia is only a beginner, I don't see what you have to worry about."

"I don't have a proper familiar either," said a voice, and a short, fat creature that looked like a furry blue pig, pushed its way forward.

Ophelia's eyes widened, though Waldorf didn't appear remotely surprised.

"Rebecca is a gimmick," explained Susannah, smiling at the blue pig. "There are very few of them left now."

"Hi!" said Rebecca cheerfully. "Look, my familiar isn't a cat either!" And with that, she pulled a fat green toad out of a pocket in her fur and held it out proudly. Gently, she stroked it with one of her long, hairy blue fingers and the toad grinned at her.

Ophelia wondered what the toad would turn into if it became human.

"Well, you're not exactly a normal witch, are you?" Beatrice went on nastily. "So you can hardly be expected to have a normal familiar."

Ophelia found it odd that a girl as pretty as Beatrice could turn so ugly whenever she opened her mouth. She looked around at the faces that now surrounded her. Some were young, some old, some strange, some beautiful, but one thing was certain: they weren't the sort of faces Ophelia would find at her old school. Some of the witches were plain with fat faces wreathed in smiles, some were like little old ladies with skinny hands and wizened features, some were too small, others too tall; and there was something odd about all of them: even the more normal-looking ones like Beatrice and Susannah carried an air of other-worldliness. Ophelia wondered if that was how children at her old school felt about *her*.

She looked over the girls' shoulders at the beds behind them, and saw for the first time that there were cats on all of them.

"That dog will frighten our cats," complained Beatrice.

"Not if he doesn't chase them," said the gimmick defensively.

Ophelia flashed her a smile of gratitude, and Waldorf padded over to one of the beds and sniffed the nose of the cat closest to him. It purred and Beatrice scowled.

"Will you be wearing different clothes tomorrow?" asked Susannah, changing the subject and looking at Ophelia's "sensible" skirt, plain white shirt and flat shoes.

Ophelia didn't know. She opened her case to see what Mrs Wolf had packed for her, and found two deep red ankle-length dresses, her hairbrush, shampoo and a toothbrush.

"My, only two dresses!" sneered Beatrice. "You're not thinking of staying long, are you? I suppose you're already expecting to be kicked out!"

Susannah glared at her. "I doubt it," she said. "Now go back to bed and leave her alone." Susannah turned her back on Beatrice. "Beatrice and Rebecca are in the room with us. So is Mabel, the large one over there."

Mabel grinned widely at this. She was enormously fat, with a smile almost as wide as her face.

"And Tracy, who is invisible."

Tracy tapped Ophelia on the shoulder and shook her hand. It was peculiar to have your hand shaken by fresh air, Ophelia thought.

In the morning, Ophelia, terrified of being late for anything, was one of the first to be up and dressed. Susannah gave her new red dress an approving look and that made her feel more confident. She smiled at the thought that Mrs Wolf had known how awkward it felt to go to a new school in the wrong uniform, though she couldn't imagine where Mrs Wolf had got the dresses from, or when.

The girls, fifteen in all, filed into a small dining room where there was a long table to one side, laden with dishes of eggs, bacon and cereal. Each of the girls was followed by her familiar, except Rebecca, who still carried her toad in her pocket.

On the table of food was a stack of plates, a stack of bowls and a stack of small tin dishes. Watching carefully to see how the other girls behaved, Ophelia saw each of them in turn take a tray from one end of the table and move further along to be served by the two ladies who stood behind it. It seemed they could have what they wanted, but each of them also picked up a small tin dish and held it out for a serving of what looked like beef stew.

Ophelia did the same. The woman serving her smiled. "You're new here, aren't you?" she asked, and peered over the table to see what Ophelia's familiar was like. When she saw Waldorf she put a second ladleful of stew into the dish Ophelia was holding out. "He needs a bit more than a cat," explained the woman.

The girls sat along the length of another table and each put her tin dish under her chair so that her cat could eat. Except Rebecca, who had a tiny dish of dead flies and insisted her toad ate them at the table, on the grounds that he could easily be stepped on.

The first class was taken by Mr Havelock. He had wild white hair, a skinny body and an unfortunate hump. He was also incredibly clumsy. He tripped over his own feet on the way to his desk at the front of the class, and sent a small spell scattering in all directions in the form of a dozen marble-sized, six-legged purple creatures whose bodies were covered in fur.

"Come on girls!" he cried, "we have to find them before they get away!"

"Why can't we just leave them?" asked Mabel, who really couldn't be bothered to exert herself.

Mr Havelock's eyes widened behind his steel-rimmed spectacles. "Do you know what happens to these things if they get fed?" he asked in horror, but he didn't enlighten them further.

The girls spent the next half hour looking for the little creatures, found eleven of them, but eventually had to give up the search for the twelfth and get on with their lesson.

The lesson was levitation. "We have to do this before we can fly, don't we girls?" said Mr Havelock brightly. "After all, there's no point in being able to fly while you're still on the ground, is there?" He rubbed his hands together in anticipation. "I love this lesson," he muttered, "it's so peaceful."

Ophelia soon saw why. In order to levitate they had to concentrate, and in order to concentrate they had to keep their eyes shut, or fix them on a distant point on the far side of the room.

"Now," instructed Mr Havelock, "think, and think hard."

For this, the girls were all sitting on the floor with their legs crossed.

"What do we think of?" asked Beatrice.

"Of levitation of course!" cried Mr Havelock gleefully. "Of floating and leaving the floor behind, of becoming weightless, of raising your body from the ground in a vertical fashion."

"I wish I thought it was as easy as he seems to," muttered the enormous Mabel.

"She's from the fat family," whispered Rebecca, who was sitting close to Ophelia. "If they're not fat, they're thrown out of the house and disinherited."

"*Quiet!*" shouted Mr Havelock suddenly, glaring at the gimmick. "For this there must be *total* silence."

Waldorf was sitting at the side of the room with the cats, watching with interest as Mabel succeeded in raising herself about six inches off the ground.

"You're doing well, Mabel," said Mr Havelock encouragingly.

Mabel, who had shut her eyes for the effort, opened them to see how high she was, and immediately fell like a stone.

"How do you expect to get anywhere if you fall whenever you open your eyes?" cried the old man. "If you can't do it with your eyes open, don't try. We'll learn how to do that next time."

Ophelia thought of what it would be like to weigh nothing at all. The harder she thought the lighter she felt and then, slowly, she felt the pressure of the floorboards lessen until she couldn't feel them at all. She kept her eyes tightly shut all the time: she didn't want to follow Mabel's example.

"Ophelia, that's quite enough, dear," said Mr Havelock nervously. "I think you can stop now."

Ophelia was tempted to open her eyes and see why, but she resisted the urge. She kept reminding herself that she weighed nothing, nothing at all.

Something touched her head, gently at first, then the pressure increased. Mr Havelock was still talking but she couldn't tell what he was saying because she was thinking so hard.

Keeping in her mind the idea that she was lighter than a feather, she decided to try opening her eyes. If she was any distance from the floor, it would be worth the bruises just to see how far. First she opened her left eye, slowly. The room looked different. She opened her other eye. Why was her face so warm? she wondered.

Ophelia turned her head, ever so slightly, and came face to face with the ceiling light. She wanted to ask how to get down again, but she was scared that if she spoke, she would break her concentration and fall. The others bobbed about below her, at various heights in the room. She could see that Mr Havelock was balding on top.

"Er, Ophelia," said Mr Havelock, "try imagining you are as light as a feather and about to eat a large plateful of meatballs, yes, meatballs should do the trick – heavier than those little sponge cakes. Now, Ophelia, you must imagine you are eating the meatballs one by one, and each one you eat makes you feel a little more full and a little heavier."

Ophelia did as she was told. And sure enough, every time she ate an imaginary meatball, she dropped a fraction from the ceiling.

"Now," said Mr Havelock, "you are about two feet from the floor. Gently stretch a leg down until you touch it."

Ophelia did so. Then she lowered her other leg and breathed a sigh of relief: concentrating that hard made her head hurt.

Everyone began to clap and Ophelia blushed. Mr Havelock said he had never seen a total beginner do so well before.

"She's nothing more than a show-off,"

snapped Beatrice. "Besides, I bet she's done all this before. She's a natural, so it's easy for her."

The class turned their heads towards Beatrice.

"How did you know?" demanded Susannah.

Beatrice went scarlet and refused to answer.

"You're simply jealous," said Mr Havelock sternly, "and it doesn't become you. Just because you're a little on the lazy side yourself, you don't like to see other people putting some effort into things and doing them better than you. Now you have some competition, perhaps you'll try harder."

Ophelia winced. Now Beatrice would resent her more than ever.

The next class was taken by Miss Wade. Miss Wade was young, short, dumpy and plain. She wore ridiculous sequinned glasses and her hair was scraped back in a tight pony tail. It was her job to teach "home economics".

"Is that cookery?" Ophelia asked Mabel, whose face was alight at the prospect. Mabel nodded, and her three chins wobbled in unison.

"Yes, my best subject," she grinned, "because the spells are all edible."

They were in a different classroom, its walls

lined with cookers and work surfaces. On each work surface in between each cooker, was a selection of bottles and jars all with neatly typed labels.

"All of you, with the exception of Tracy, are to work in pairs. We're going to learn the rudiments of concocting an invisibility potion," announced Miss Wade, "and, of course, the antidote. After all, there's no point in the one without the other."

Mabel was paired off with Ophelia.

"Where's Tracy?" Ophelia whispered.

"If you look hard at that wall over there," replied Mabel, "you'll see that part of it is slightly blurred. Well, that's where Tracy is standing. It's fortunate she's so shy or she could play the most terrible tricks on us. The invisibility antidote doesn't work on her."

"Come on girls, stop talking," demanded Miss Wade in a rather timid voice, pushing her glasses further back on her nose with her forefinger. "Now, each pair take a small saucepan from beside your cooker. That's right. Measure out half a teaspoon of saxifrage powder, one pint of water, a pinch of salt and six drops of lizard essence. Bring to the boil – I hope you're taking notes – then, while one of you stirs, the other must grind down two segments of rabbit backbone with the mortar and pestle, and add it to the mixture."

Ophelia stared apprehensively at the souplike potion in front of her.

"Come on, Ophelia, what are you waiting for?" cried Miss Wade. "Pour your share into a glass and drink it!"

Ophelia shut her eyes and swallowed the invisibility mixture in one go.

She didn't feel any different, but when she looked down at her fingers and saw they weren't there she became terribly dizzy. It made the floor seem curiously close, to know her hands were outstretched above it at a height she could no longer judge.

"I know I've forgotten something important," muttered Miss Wade, tapping her chin thoughtfully. "I just can't remember what it is."

Somebody unzipped the back of Miss Wade's dress and pulled it down to her waist and elbows, to reveal a very tight, old-fashioned corset – the kind that held *everything* in.

"Now I remember!" she cried, pulling her dress back up again. She reached for one of the girl's saucepans and drank the dregs of the invisibility mixture. Within a moment she had vanished, and she let out a sigh of relief. Now no one could see her to torment her, and the lesson continued with instructions on the antidote.

Ophelia poured her antidote into a glass and was about to drink it, when the glass was knocked violently out of her hand and smashed on the floor.

One by one the other girls became visible. Beatrice reappeared last, and she was smiling.

"Ophelia," called Miss Wade, "where are you?"

"Over here, Miss Wade. I'm afraid I dropped my antidote," Ophelia said quietly.

"Oh dear, oh dear," twittered Miss Wade. "We'll have to make some more and Miss Rose is bound to find out! If you're not in time for lunch she'll know something is wrong, and even *I* can't make antidote that quickly."

"Why the fuss? Would Miss Rose be angry?" Ophelia asked Mabel, remembering the small, kind, plump woman.

"Oh yes," answered Mabel. "She's nice when it suits her, but she has a terrible temper, and she's a stickler for time-keeping and rules. I'm sure it was Beatrice who knocked the glass out of your hand." Ophelia thought so too.

A second later a jug of water upended itself over Beatrice's head, plastering her hair to the sides of her face and instantly soaking through her white cotton dress.

The class burst into hysterical giggles.

"I didn't know she had it in her," whispered Susannah to Mabel with a grin.

"Who did that?" demanded Miss Wade. "Ophelia, it must have been you!"

"Miss Wade," said Susannah in her clear voice, "did you actually *see* Ophelia pour the water?"

Miss Wade looked puzzled for a moment, then admitted she hadn't.

"It was an accident, the same way Ophelia dropping her glass was an accident," Susannah explained.

"I see," sighed Miss Wade. "All right, class dismissed. Ophelia, you stay with me and we'll make you visible again as quickly as possible."

"I must do it myself," insisted Ophelia. "I have to learn and I'll learn faster that way."

Ophelia, visible once more, ran into the dining room with Waldorf at her heels, to find everyone already seated with their food in front of them and their familiars under their chairs.

"Come and sit with us," called Rebecca the gimmick. "We've saved you a seat." She was sitting with Susannah, Mabel and Tracy. Beatrice sat a little further down the table with two girls from the other dormitory, and still looked a little damp.

As soon as the meal was over, Miss Rose walked into the dining room and came straight over to Ophelia.

"Ophelia," she said sternly, "please would you come with me. I'd like to talk to you before lessons begin this afternoon."

"Oh no," whispered Rebecca, "she must have found out about the spilt antidote."

Miss Rose took Ophelia and Waldorf to her room and sat them down in front of her desk.

"Why were you late for lunch?" she asked Ophelia.

"I dropped my glass of invisibility potion," replied Ophelia. Somehow, she couldn't bear to tell tales on Beatrice, even if she did deserve it.

"Rubbish, it was Beatrice, wasn't it?" snapped Miss Rose.

Ophelia stared.

"Oh, it's all right, you're not in danger of telling tales, but the girl is a lazy so-and-so, and it doesn't require a genius to see that she's taken a dislike to you. I'd have a word with her parents about her attitude, if I only knew who they were." Miss Rose smiled at the expression of surprise on Ophelia's face.

"Our parents are usually anonymous," she explained. "Now, I'll tell you the real reason why I wanted to see you, although I'd appreciate it if you allowed the others, especially Beatrice, to think it was in order to punish you. I wanted to ask if you would like extra tuition. Mrs Wolf explained the gravity of your grandmother's situation, and I understand you only have three weeks left before it's too late.'

Ophelia's face lit up. "I'd love extra lessons!" she cried. "Anything to learn quickly. But three weeks is only a rough guess; it might be a lot less."

"I'm afraid it's impossible to teach you enough to enable you to help your grandmother in less time than that," said Miss Rose. "Though if you worked day and night you might be able to leave in, say, two weeks; but we couldn't allow that."

Ophelia hung her head and decided she *would* work day and night.

"Now, my dear, every afternoon there is a two-hour break before the lessons begin. So I would like you to come here to my room, the moment you've finished lunch, and we will practise everything you've learned before the break. Until you are perfect."

Miss Rose was as good as her word and by the time the rest period was over, Ophelia was exhausted.

"Just tell the others you have three weeks'

detention with me," instructed Miss Rose as Ophelia was leaving.

Ophelia woke rather late the next morning and found that everyone else was almost dressed. Hurriedly, she slipped into her own dress, only to discover that someone had cut holes in it. She looked around the room for Beatrice, but Beatrice had already left.

"Quickly, put on your other one," said Susannah. "We'll have to see you in the dining room or we'll all be late."

Left alone, Ophelia changed into her other dress. But that had been slashed too.

"I'll have to fix them somehow, and quickly," she said to Waldorf. "But I'm not sure how. I have to think. Magic isn't so much learning a spell as learning how to think, and wishing."

She lay the dresses side by side on the bed. Then, feeling a little self-conscious in front of Waldorf, she rested her right index finger at one end of a tear, half closed her eyes and willed the material to mend. She concentrated so hard her temples hurt. Then she drew her finger down the length of the tear.

"It's going together like a zip!" announced Waldorf.

Faster and faster Ophelia ran her finger over one tear after another. Where a whole piece had been cut out, she passed her hand over the hole and sealed it. Though she instinctively felt that she *could* do it, she was no less astonished at her success.

She and Waldorf walked into the dining room just in time to join the end of the breakfast queue. Everyone thought Ophelia was wearing her spare dress – except Beatrice, who dropped her breakfast tray and stood gaping.

At the end of the fifth day Waldorf was getting worried. "You never stop," he complained. "Don't you think that working in the bathroom while everyone else is asleep is overdoing it a little?"

Ophelia was sitting on the edge of one of the bathtubs with a pile of magic books at her feet and one open on her lap.

"I agree with Waldorf," said a voice from the doorway.

Ophelia froze. But it was only Susannah.

"Miss Rose asked me to keep a special eye on you and now I know why. You'll make yourself ill if you go on like this; then you won't be any use to anybody. Miss Rose told me you have another two weeks before you go home to your grandmother. Can't you take things a little more easily?"

Ophelia shook her head. "It could be less than that before Gran disappears completely," she replied. "So I want to leave as soon as possible. Anyway, now that you know Waldorf can talk, I suppose I'll *have* to leave."

"It does usually mean an animal can take on human form." Susannah smiled. "But since I'm the only one who knows about it, you needn't worry. Just as long as he doesn't turn into a boy while he's still here."

"Er, I don't even know if I can," lied Waldorf. "I've never tried."

"You should have told me how you felt," Susannah went on. "If you're not powerful enough to get rid of your visitors by the time you leave – and you won't be, of course – then more than one of us might be."

Ophelia stared at her in surprise.

"The more people you have to help, the sooner you can leave," said Susannah. "I'll see how many of the others would like to come with us when we go."

"Will the others want to help?" asked Ophelia. "Like Beatrice said, I'm not really one of you. Look at you, for instance: you seem like a real witch to me; and you're so good at everything you do."

"But you're better," pointed out Susannah, "and you're still only a beginner."

Ophelia gave her a grateful smile.

"All we have to do is find a way for a few of us to go missing without anyone else noticing," Susannah went on. "If Miss Rose found out that a group of half-trained pupils were going off to take on two practising witches, she'd go mad.

After all, while we're here, we are her responsibility."

Waldorf sniffed the air. There was a sour smell. He knew he'd smelt it before but had to struggle to remember where. Then he had it: it was the same scent he'd detected on the night they arrived. He cleared his throat and nodded towards the door. The two girls fell silent and followed his gaze.

They heard the faint rustle of a dress on the floor outside the bathroom, then light footsteps retreating down the hall.

"I'm sure it was Beatrice," whispered Waldorf, "because I smelt the same smell outside Miss Rose's room when we first arrived. And remember, Beatrice knew Ophelia was a natural when only Susannah had been told. She must have been listening outside the door."

"So *that*'s why she was still dressed that night," muttered Susannah.

"Oh dear," sighed Ophelia, "now she knows what we're planning to do. I don't know why she feels about me the way she does, but you can be sure she'll try to stop us."

Susannah tapped the side of her nose and smiled broadly. "Just leave it to me. By the time I've arranged things, she can tell Miss Rose what she likes, but everything will look normal and

Beatrice will look a fool."

"How long do you think it will be before we can leave, then?" asked Ophelia hopefully.

"I think you should take a day to go over everything you've learned," advised Susannah. "Then you can show me what you're capable of. I just want to make sure you can look after yourself. If you pass my 'test', we'll leave the following evening – so you'll only have been here for a week. Will that suit you?"

Ophelia said it certainly would.

The following day, Ophelia spent all her time in between classes practising everything she knew.

"Remember," said Waldorf, "it's better to know a few things well than only a little of many things."

That night, when the others were all asleep, Susannah led Ophelia and Waldorf into the empty cookery classroom. "All right, Ophelia," she said, "I want you to show me everything you can do."

Waldorf crept into a corner and hoped Susannah was going to be as surprised as he had been.

Ophelia let out a deep breath and then began. She raised herself from the floor and flew around the room with great control. "I've got

this far," she told Susannah, "but I never know whether to do it sitting or lying down."

"Start sitting and finish lying on your front," said Susannah practically.

Then Susannah threw some streaks of lightning and several small round lead marbles at Ophelia from the palm of her hand. Ophelia concentrated on the idea of being surrounded by a blue glow. Gradually her skin turned blue and began to shine. The light got stronger and stronger, and the bolts and lead balls bounced off the edge of it with such force that they embedded themselves in the walls.

"Stop!" cried Susannah.

Ophelia stopped and Susannah rubbed her eyes. "That's amazing!" she exclaimed. "The light was so bright I could hardly see you. Your normal unconscious protection must be phenomenal."

"I hope it is, for her sake," muttered Waldorf.

Ophelia proceeded to surprise even herself. She grew spaghetti from the ends of her fingers; she made flames dance on her fingertips (though the thumbs kept going out); she made Waldorf levitate, and willed herself to look like Mary. She succeeded in creating a face very like Mary's, though the moment she stopped concentrating, it vanished.

Then Ophelia did the most surprising thing – she disappeared.

"Hey!" cried Susannah. "We haven't learnt yet how to make ourselves vanish and reappear somewhere else. That's for experts."

"I haven't appeared anywhere else," said Ophelia's voice.

"But you can't be invisible without the invisibility potion. Did you have a bottle of it on you?"

Ophelia laughed. "You didn't see me drink anything, did you?"

Susannah shook her head.

"Well, there you are," said Ophelia. "Actually,

I worked this out for myself. I can't become invisible without the potion, and I can't move from place to place without being seen, so I imagined the room behind me to be in front of me. What you're seeing is what's behind me. It has the same effect as being invisible, though I'm not really invisible at all. If you walk round me, I'll slowly become visible to you again."

Susannah put her hand over her open mouth. For a moment she was at a loss for words. "But that's the most wonderful idea!" she cried. "Good grief, I would say you're as ready to face Mary as you're ever going to be."

Chapter Five

It was time for them to leave. Susannah met Ophelia in the bathroom after "lights out". "I had to put a little sleep spell on Beatrice," she told Ophelia, "just to make sure she doesn't wake until she's supposed to, tomorrow morning."

The bathroom door opened suddenly and Waldorf began to growl. It was Miss Wade. She stood in the doorway eyeing Waldorf with distrust, wearing nothing but a long white nightgown. Her hair was loose and hanging straight down her back but she still wore her sequinned glasses. She was blushing deeply.

Ophelia gasped in dismay.

"It's all right, Ophelia. I asked her to meet us here," explained Susannah.

"You did say it was life or death," said Miss

Wade timidly, "or I'd never have come."

"We need your help to cover up the fact that tomorrow a few of us won't be here," Susannah told her.

Miss Wade collapsed on to the edge of the bath. "I can't possibly do that!" she protested. "If Miss Rose ever found out I'd helped you skip school without permission, she'd sack me! I'd never get another job again. I'd be blacklisted. I'd have to become a black witch just to make a living, and it's really not in my nature to be nasty, you know."

"Ophelia," interrupted Waldorf, making Miss Wade jump with surprise, "tell her the story and she might see things in a different light."

Ophelia told her story all over again.

"Beatrice is the only one who would give us away," Susannah added when Ophelia had finished, "and she won't wake up until the early hours of the morning, so you don't have to worry about her until then."

Much later, Ophelia, Waldorf and Susannah were creeping through the underground school passages, followed by Tracy the invisible girl, Rebecca the gimmick and Mabel the fat girl. All the way up the long entrance hall Ophelia imagined Miss Rose's voice bellowing after

126

them: "And where do you think you're going?"

But they reached the door to the telephone exchange safely and stepped out into the cold night air.

Ophelia tucked Waldorf firmly under one arm.

"It looks as though we're on our way," cried Susannah. "Come on, everybody!"

One by one they rose from the ground, not all with equal grace or ease. There was the occasional giggle as the breeze overturned them slightly, or they bumped over a pocket of air.

When they reached the house Ophelia led them silently round to her own bedroom window. Inside, the light was on, and the toy Ophelia and Waldorf were sitting motionless on the bed beside Mrs Wolf, who was flipping through a mammoth book on witchcraft.

Waldorf knocked at the window and Mrs Wolf looked up in surprise. At the sight of Ophelia floating outside, she hurried to the window and threw it open. "Good grief!" she exclaimed. "I would never have believed you could learn to do that in such a short time, if I hadn't seen it with my own eyes! I wasn't expecting you until at least the end of the week."

She was even more surprised when Susannah, Rebecca and Mabel flew up behind Ophelia and followed her into the room. She couldn't see Tracy and shut the window before she could get in. Tracy knocked loudly and Mrs Wolf opened the window again. "Thank you," said a small voice. It was the first time Ophelia had heard Tracy speak.

"I see you've brought the cavalry," Mrs Wolf said with a broad smile.

"Surely, together we must have some chance of getting rid of Mary, Blackie and Veronica?" Ophelia asked.

"You certainly have," replied Mrs Wolf. "Though I can tell you, when your grandmother wakes up and sees what they've done to her house, she'll want to go straight back to bed again! I've been kept on my toes while you were gone, and I've done by best to keep the chaos contained in the kitchen. Those creatures downstairs seem to live, eat and sleep in the kitchen now."

"Is the Doctor all right?" Ophelia wanted to know.

"Oh yes," said Mrs Wolf, "except that Mary's been throwing some of the stuff they concoct out into the garden, and it makes the grass and weeds grow like crazy. The Doctor's fine when

I can find him, but now you're here, I might have time to go out and trim around him a little." She waved her hands over the Ophelia and Waldorf look-alikes and they returned to their original size and appearance with a hiss of escaping air.

The first thing Ophelia wanted to do was to see her grandmother and Mrs Wolf led her along the corridor and into Gran's room. The door to the room stood permanently ajar now as Mary no longer had to bother about hiding the evidence of her activities.

Ophelia's grandmother seemed to have withered away. The little heap under the bedclothes had sunk lower into the mattress than the plaster cast on her leg, and she looked as brittle and transparent as glass, her veins and most of her bones now clearly visible. Through her body Ophelia could see some of the creases in the sheet beneath her and she burst into tears.

"Oh my," said Susannah, keeping a respectful distance in the doorway. "I think we'd better get to work as soon as possible." The girls standing behind her nodded their agreement. They were silent and subdued.

Mrs Wolf ushered the girls downstairs and left them in the living room, taking Ophelia and Waldorf to the kitchen with her.

Ophelia couldn't help but notice the thick, cloying smell that hung in the air, reminding her of rotting cabbages. Inside the kitchen the smell was overpowering.

Blackie was toying with a dish of mixed insects that weren't yet dead, and Mary and Veronica were playing a game of draughts using dead cockroaches. They took absolutely no notice of Mrs Wolf.

"Do you have to take that dog everywhere with you, Ophelia?" asked Mary in a bored voice. "Blackie's wearing a path over the windowsill."

The fake Waldorf and Ophelia had obviously been keeping up appearances.

"Don't you remember, Mary? Ophelia's sent us to Coventry," said Veronica. "A whole week without speech. Quite a feat."

Ophelia looked around her. There was a real cat under the table: clearly Veronica's familiar. A small snake had wrapped itself round one of the chair legs. The windowsill was sprouting a thick coat of green fungus that still held cat footprints and the floor was covered in variously coloured slime from spilt concoctions. The sink was invisible beneath a pile of utensils that overflowed on to both sides of the worktop. The wallpaper was peeling from the walls with the heat and steam; the cooker was caked in black, burnt liquid out of which protruded evidence of half-cooked objects; three of the cupboard doors were missing, and one of the shelves on which Gran kept her preserves dangled down the wall, its contents crushed and oozing at the bottom among the pile of broken glass jars.

A large wolf spider picked its way among the debris and got stuck in a puddle of something sticky. Absent-mindedly, Mary bent down, picked it up and popped it in her mouth with a small crunch. Ophelia swallowed her desire to be sick as the spider's legs twitched between Mary's lips and disappeared.

"Come on, Ophelia," said Mrs Wolf quietly. "There's nothing we can do here, yet."

"There's nothing you can do here at *any* time," retorted Mary.

Mrs Wolf caught Ophelia by the wrist and pulled her out of the kitchen, just as Ophelia was thinking of setting light to the draughtboard with fire from her fingers. She

could almost smell the toasted cockroaches, and see the look of astonishment on Mary's horrible imitation of Grandmother's face.

"I think we'd better join the others in the living room to decide what we should do first," whispered Mrs Wolf, "before you show Mary what you're capable of."

They had no sooner reached the living room than there was a sudden shattering sound and a shower of glass as a figure burst through the French windows. Everyone ducked and Tracy screamed.

Ophelia lifted her head to see Mr Havelock standing just inside the room, brushing glass splinters off his slightly shabby suit.

"Susannah," hissed Ophelia, "we've been followed!"

Susannah looked up from beneath the cushion she had used to cover her head.

"Mr Havelock!" she cried. "What on earth are you doing here? Have you come to take us back? Have they already discovered we've gone?"

Mr Havelock raised his hand against this barrage of questions. "Nothing of the kind," he told her. "But I've known Miss Wade too long for her to be able to lie to me. I met her in the corridor after she talked to you and I knew she was trying to cover something up, so I've been following you ever since."

"Did you have to break the window?" asked Ophelia plaintively.

"Oh, I'm sorry about that, dear," muttered Mr Havelock sheepishly. "I really have a problem on these short runway stops, you know." He brushed some more glass off his jacket and a shower of gold dust fluttered through the air: his spells were leaking again.

"If Miss Rose ever finds out about your escapade," he continued, "she'll feel a lot better in knowing there was a responsible member of staff present. Then she'll sack me, of course."

"I don't know if I'd call *him* responsible," giggled Tracy in Ophelia's ear. She had a voice like a mouse.

Ophelia was about to ask Mrs Wolf how she thought they could best employ their numbers in fighting Veronica and Mary, when there was an explosion and the living room door fell inwards. The two black witches stood in the doorway.

"Why can't you open the door like normal people?" snapped Mrs Wolf.

They ignored her.

"So this is what's going on," sneered Mary. "Little Ophelia has brought some friends round for a tea party. I didn't think she had any."

Veronica threw back her head and roared with laughter.

"Look at that one!" she howled, pointing at Rebecca. "It looks like a blue blimp!"

Furious, Rebecca got to her feet, but Waldorf pulled her back by her fur.

"Not yet," he told her. "Wait a while."

"Come on, Veronica," said Mary, "let's get back to the kitchen. There's nothing a group of scruffy kids and a couple of old-age pensioners can do to us."

For a second, Ophelia held her tongue, but she was boiling with anger and knew that if she hesitated, her courage would be gone. "I've had *enough*!" she shouted, and sent a bolt of blue light from her mouth as she spoke.

No one moved: none of them had ever seen that happen before – any more than Ophelia had. Veronica and Mary backed out of the doorway. Then, to Ophelia's astonishment, they turned and ran back to the kitchen.

"We've got to catch them!" cried Ophelia, running after them.

"Oh dear, I wasn't quite ready for this," panted Mrs Wolf. "Come on, Waldorf, we've got to stop her before they do anything to her."

"I don't think they can," gasped Waldorf.

"She's learnt how to look after herself now."

They swung open the kitchen door just in time to see Ophelia upend a bowl of pink stew over Blackie's head. Blackie let out a howl and tried to rub the mess out of her eyes, but invisible Tracy grabbed her hands, pulled them behind her back and tied them with a dirty dishcloth.

Mary and Veronica yelled invisibility antidote spells, but they had no effect because Tracy, of course, wasn't under a spell.

"Throw something that'll stick to her!" screamed Mary.

Veronica thrust her hand into a bowl on the table and scooped out a lump of jellied flies which she threw towards the place where she imagined Tracy was standing. The jellied flies splattered against the far wall. Mary threw a pan of soup and the same thing happened.

"That's no good," screeched Veronica, "we don't know where she is now!"

She began throwing handfuls of jellied flies around the room at random, and Mary did the same with panfuls of green liquid. It was too much for Tracy, who started to laugh. Mary threw a handful of green in the direction of the laugh and caught Tracy full in the face. For a moment, everyone stared. Tracy's features were outlined in brilliant green. Ophelia could see that she wasn't a young girl at all: she was an old woman, and small, like a dwarf.

"Don't stand there gawping!" Mary shouted at Veronica. "*Get her!*"

Still laughing, Tracy pushed past Ophelia and Mrs Wolf. "It's up to you now," she giggled. "I'm off to wash my face."

The last Ophelia saw of her was an enormous hooked nose and a pointed chin, bobbing through the air as she took the stairs two at a time.

Mary and Veronica didn't bother to chase her: they had more to worry about close at hand.

Blackie, meanwhile, was still wailing loudly, and nosing between Ophelia and Mrs Wolf, Waldorf saw his chance. He bounded across the floor and landed in Blackie's lap. It was more than the girl could stand. She unglued herself from her chair and walked unsteadily to the open back door, where she struggled free from the dishcloth, dropped to her hands and knees and stumbled into the garden. Using the Doctor's sleeping form as a ladder, she climbed up into the apple tree and refused to budge.

"Come back here, you rotten, lousy, stinking cat!" screamed Mary. "You know I'm not as strong without you. What do you think familiars are for?"

"They shouldn't beee subjected to what isssss happening heeeeere," hissed Blackie. "Consider meeeee on strike!"

A long gey tail dropped down from beneath her skirt, so Waldorf bit the end of it, causing another howl. He returned to the kitchen just in time to see Mary throw a spell from her fingertips at Ophelia. "Duck!" he shouted, forgetting Ophelia's natural protection. Automatically, she did so, and the spell hit Rebecca, who was standing just behind her. Rebecca's self-protection was almost non-existent and she immediately turned into a turtle.

"Quick," said Mrs Wolf, "we have to change her back!"

But Ophelia was so stunned by the speed of the activity taking place around her, she couldn't remember the words that returned spellbound objects to their original form. Mrs Wolf lunged forward and grabbed Veronica by the arm, before she could stamp on the turtle. As she did so, Veronica changed herself into a giant python which fell to the floor and curled around the turtle. The python began to squeeze. Susannah and Mabel desperately tried to uncoil it but it was too strong.

Ophelia realised that there was no point in turning Rebecca back into a gimmick, because a gimmick could still be crushed by the steel grip she was in. Just in time she remembered another spell. She used it now on Rebecca, and Rebecca turned into a cannonball like the one in the Doctor's study, only much, much bigger. It had been the first non-breakable thing Ophelia could think of.

"Ooops," she said, "I didn't mean it to be quite so big."

Mary was following Ophelia around the kitchen table chanting a spell, but the words that came out of her mouth had no effect. Susannah and Mr Havelock caught hold of her arms and dragged her to the floor, where Mabel sat on her so she couldn't move.

The snake came slithering after the steel ball, which had begun to roll away, opened its mouth wide and disconnected its jaws so that it could swallow the ball more easily.

Rebecca disappeared halfway down the snake's throat.

"Veronica's going to realise she made a big mistake," said Mrs Wolf with a grin.

She was right. The snake couldn't move with the weight of the steel ball inside her, and couldn't speak because the ball wasn't far enough down her throat.

Mrs Wolf bent down and shouted into the snake's open mouth: "Could you stay put for a few minutes, Rebecca? Only Veronica can't change back into human form while you're there, because you'd still be stuck in her throat and she'd choke."

"Anything to oblige," answered a muffled voice.

The snake tried to regurgitate the ball, but it was far too heavy and awkward: Veronica was well and truly immobilised.

Mr Havelock tried to produce a gag for Mary to stop her performing magic.

"Please be quick," begged Susannah, who had her hand over Mary's mouth and was in danger of getting her fingers bitten off.

Mr Havelock muttered something and produced a tatty-looking pony out of thin air.

"They wanted a gag, not a nag," said Mrs Wolf, grabbing a filthy tea towel from the floor and tying it around the lower part of Mary's face.

"Now we need a rope," cried Mabel as Mary's bulk heaved beneath her. She waved her hand in the air and out of the end of her forefinger came a long, thin piece of string. It got longer and longer as she zigzagged her hand from side to side. Susannah took the end of it and wrapped it tightly around Mary's wrists while Ophelia held them together in front of Mary's face.

"Got a pair of scissors?" Mabel asked Ophelia.

Ophelia licked her fingers and blew on them, and her right index and middle finger became a pair of scissors. She cut the string from Mabel's finger, then blew on her own again to return them to normal.

Mary was now bound and gagged, and Veronica was immobile with Rebecca stuck in her throat. "Umphght grugh," she said nastily.

"Well, so far, so good," sighed Mrs Wolf, wiping the grime from her hands down the sides of the rather nice skirt she was wearing. "But I'm a little amazed. It's been easier than I expected."

"I'm not complaining," grinned Ophelia, wiping the sweat from her forehead and glancing down at Mary's prostrate form. "But I suppose we have to think of something to do with them now, and we have to make sure that whatever it is, they won't come back."

"It's the last bit that's going to be difficult," admitted Mrs Wolf. "Mary will want to get her own back on you any way she can after this."

Mr Havelock, meanwhile, had been trying to get rid of the scruffy pony and had so far only succeeded in turning it bright red and getting his spells completely stuck. In total frustration he kept shaking his hands and staring accusingly at the ends of his fingers. Eventually, he gave up and pushed the pony out of the back door into the garden.

"I think," said Mrs Wolf, addressing Susannah, Mabel and Tracy, who had cleaned her face off and was invisible again, "that the situation is quite under contol now. So, once we've got Rebecca out of Veronica's mouth, you can go back to school. In fact, if you're quick, you might get back before anyone wakes up."

"I doubt it," Susannah said. "Look, it's getting light already."

She was right. Dawn was beginning to creep across the sky.

"We have no time to lose then," cried Mrs Wolf. "The sooner you go back, the less chance there is of your absence, or Miss Wade's efforts to conceal it, being discovered."

She reached into the bowl of jellied flies and scooped out a handful. Lifting Veronica's top jaw, she smeared jelly all over the steel ball, turned it and smeared on some more. Having done this to her satisfaction, she stamped on the snake's neck, just behind the steel ball and the ball popped out, landing on the floor with a

heavy thud.

The snake immediately turned back into Veronica, coughing and spluttering and holding her throat.

"You'll regret that," she growled hoarsely.

"Why should she?" asked Ophelia angrily. "She saved you from choking."

Veronica pointed at Mrs Wolf and began muttering under her breath. As she muttered Mrs Wolf was engulfed in a blue glow.

"I wish I could do that," said Mabel admiringly. "I haven't learnt how to yet."

She and Tracy joined hands and concentrated

on returning Rebecca to her usual form.

"I can't believe I let myself get caught like that," complained the gimmick, trying to pick all the jellied flies out of her fur.

"Do you think you might leave now?" Ophelia asked Veronica, who had given up trying to bewitch Mrs Wolf and was leaning against the kitchen table panting.

"Never!" she gasped in a cracked voice. "I live here now and there's nothing you can do about it; and as long as we're here, Mary and I, you'll never get your grandmother back! In fact, in two days' time, she'll have vanished altogether! Hah!"

Veronica was about to go and untie Mary, when she found herself surrounded by Ophelia, Tracy, Susannah, Rebecca, Mrs Wolf and Mr Havelock.

Mrs Wolf began to chant a rhyme that sounded vaguely familiar to Ophelia. Then she remembered it was the spell Miss Walton the white witch had tried to use when shrinking Blackie to get her into the bird cage.

One by one the girls picked up the words and joined in. Veronica began to plead, then she began to beg. "Please, no, no! Don't do that," she whimpered. Frantically, she tried to protect herself with her own blue light, but as fast as the blue light wrapped itself around her, it disintegrated in loose coils at her feet. She tried to push her way between her antagonists, but they stood fast and pushed her back into the middle of the circle.

Veronica put her hands up as if to protect her face. She was getting smaller and smaller and her pleas were growing fainter and fainter. Now she was the same size as Waldorf; now she was the size of a small cat; now she was no bigger than a matchbox.

When are we going to stop? Ophelia wondered. Then she realised they *weren't* going to stop, because as long as Veronica was big enough to have a voice, she could make magic to break the spell the moment they stopped chanting. She was now the size of a peanut.

"That's it!" cried Mrs Wolf above the other voices. "We're nearly there."

"Small, small, out of sight and out of mind, small, small, too small to find," they chanted.

The peanut-sized Veronica made one last attempt to escape, but Mrs Wolf caught her on the toe of her shoe and tossed her back into the middle of the circle. There was a small "pop" and Veronica vanished altogether.

Suddenly, there was complete silence. Even Mary stopped struggling and went quiet.

Chapter Six

Back at school Beatrice had woken up. She had left the girls apparently lying in their beds and gone to tell Miss Rose how they were planning to get out one night; and, moreover, that Waldorf could talk.

Now Miss Rose was letting her out of one of the correction rooms. "You're very fortunate I couldn't think of something worse," she was saying. "I dislike telltales even more than I dislike broken rules."

"There was nothing to look at but mirrors!" wailed Beatrice, who could normally spend hours in front of one.

"It should teach you not to be so vain and have such a high regard for yourself," retorted Miss Rose.

"I never want to see myself in a mirror again," whined Beatrice. It's all Ophelia's fault, she told herself bitterly; and the bitterness chewed away inside her and grew.

"Now," said Miss Rose, "go in and join the others. They're in lessons now; they haven't gone anywhere yet."

"But I heard them say they were going to," protested Beatrice.

Miss Rose frowned at her and she fell silent.

Beatrice found morning lessons were being taken by Miss Wade instead of Mr Havelock. "Mr Havelock is ill," explained Miss Wade, with rather more conviction than she could normally muster when telling the truth. She disliked Beatrice intensely. Beatrice always made her feel ugly and foolish.

Beatrice took her place beside Susannah. "I hope you're happy now," she hissed. "I've missed breakfast, and been punished for telling on you and your little friend! But I'll get you back for that."

Susannah just looked at her coldly and didn't speak.

"Did you hear what I said?" demanded Beatrice.

Miss Wade told her to be quiet, but Beatrice was too angry to take any notice. She gripped Susannah by the arm, but her fingers touched only cold air. "You're freezing!" she cried, pulling her hand away.

Beatrice turned round. Ophelia, sitting in the row behind her, looked up slowly and smiled. Beatrice felt suddenly afraid. There was something wrong and she didn't know what it was. What had they been saying against her? Everything had been all right until Ophelia had come to school.

"It's all your fault!" she screamed at her, and before she could stop herself, she slapped Ophelia across the face. Ophelia continued to smile as Beatrice's hand passed right through her cheek. Beatrice stared: Ophelia was fading before her very eyes. She looked at Susannah and saw that Susannah was disappearing too. So were Mabel and Rebecca, laughing at her as they faded. The other girls in the class, the ones that weren't disappearing, were laughing too. They all knew!

"They weren't here at all!" yelled Beatrice. She felt as though she was going to explode. She looked at Miss Wade – timid, plain, boring Miss Wade, who would never say boo to a goose – and saw Miss Wade was laughing so much the tears were running down her face. Beatrice ran from the room, slamming the door behind her. Miss Wade's laughter rang in her ears all the way down the corridor.

She was stopped by Susannah, the invisible Tracy, Mabel and Rebecca.

"Where do you think you're going?" demanded Susannah.

"I'm telling Miss Rose you're not here," shouted Beatrice, pointing back to the classroom, "because this time it's true." Then she hesitated, a puzzled look on her face. She poked Rebecca and felt real, warm fur.

"But we are quite obviously here," said Rebecca with a wide smile.

Beatrice sagged momentarily, then pushed her way through them and ran back to the dormitory, where she sat plotting her revenge.

During the lunch break, she found one of the girls from the other dormitory, took her aside and wouldn't let her go until the girl had told her where Ophelia lived.

As soon as Beatrice had gone, the girl ran to Susannah to show her the bruises Beatrice had given her.

Everyone was astonished. It was one of the strictest school rules that no girl ever harm another, either physically or by magic. A witch who hurt another was a potential black witch, and the headmistress kept them out. But sometimes a witch didn't show her true colours for a while.

"Does it matter that Beatrice knows where Ophelia lives, now that you've helped her?" asked the girl nervously.

Susannah didn't know.

By the time Beatrice reached Ophelia's house she was in an even more furious mood. She'd had a very rocky flight because her flying skills were so poor, and as far as she was concerned, that was Ophelia's fault too.

Peering through the kitchen window, she saw Mr Havelock banging his hand on the kitchen table in an attempt to unstick his spells, Mary on the floor, all tied up and gagged, and Ophelia and Mrs Wolf talking to Waldorf. Making a sudden decision, she launched herself at the kitchen window, smashing it to pieces as she passed through it and using her inefficient blue glow to protect herself from cuts.

Ophelia took one look at Beatrice's contorted face and knew they were in for trouble. "There goes another of Gran's windows," she muttered under her breath.

Beatrice landed on the floor beside Mary and pulled off the gag. "Hello Mother, I've come to help," she said.

"Mother?" cried Ophelia. Everything suddenly fell into place.

"I wanted to come and warn you about Ophelia," Beatrice told Mary as she ripped off the cords at her wrists. "But you know how difficult it is to get out of school, and she was no danger while she was there and I could keep an eye on her."

Mary stood up and smiled nastily, her face covered with grease smears and gravy from the tea towel. "Stay with me, my dear, and you'll be all right."

She cupped her hands and grinned as her palms filled with fire, then threw the fireball at Ophelia.

"Think of blue light!" shouted Waldorf.

Ophelia thought of blue light and the fireball bounced off her, exploding against the kitchen wall and fizzling out in the damp.

Beatrice tried to copy Mary, but all she could produce were faintly glowing pebbles. She threw them anyway and they clattered against the blue glow like wood blocks on an empty cake tin.

Mrs Wolf launched herself at Beatrice and threw her to the floor, landing right on top of her.

Beatrice tried to throw Mrs Wolf off, but Mrs Wolf was a great deal larger than she was, and a lot heavier. No matter how much she wriggled,

Beatrice couldn't shift her.

"It's up to you now!" Mrs Wolf shouted to Ophelia. "I'll keep this one quiet, but you and Waldorf must deal with Mary."

Mary clapped her hands and threw a small black bolt in Ophelia's direction. Ophelia automatically stepped aside and the bolt headed for Mrs Wolf, who hadn't seen it and wasn't adequately protected as a result. With uncharacteristic speed, Mr Havelock pulled Mrs Wolf off Beatrice, who immediately sat up and was hit by the bolt herself. The next moment she was a chicken.

The chicken ran under the table and stood there quaking.

Mary saw that Mrs Wolf, Mr Havelock and Ophelia together would be too much for her and turned and ran out of the back door, through the garden gate and down the street, leaving Ophelia speechless with astonishment.

"I don't believe it," she said quietly. "She's gone!"

"I think she'll be back though," said Mrs Wolf grimly. "What we have to do now is get your grandmother awake before she returns. She'll want her revenge on you, you know."

Mr Havelock began to clear up the kitchen while Ophelia and Waldorf followed Mrs Wolf upstairs.

There was no doubt about it: Grandmother had almost gone.

"Please, Mrs Wolf," begged Ophelia, gazing down at the glass-like figure on the bed, "do something quickly."

Mrs Wolf pulled a handkerchief out of her pocket and flicked away the worst of the dust from the transparent old lady. She knelt by the side of the bed, took the old woman's hand in her own and began to rub it gently, muttering under her breath as she did so. Ophelia listened and understood every word. She said the words over and over again to herself so that she would never forget them.

"Now," said Mrs Wolf, "all we have to do is wait a few seconds." She stood up and checked her watch.

Five minutes later she checked it again. "I don't understand it," she said in a puzzled voice. "Your grandmother should be back to normal by now, but nothing's happening."

"You don't think we're too late, do you?" asked Ophelia breathlessly.

"Not at all," replied Mrs Wolf. "She wouldn't be here if we were too late."

"Try again," suggested Waldorf in a worried voice.

Mrs Wolf repeated her incantation and this time Ophelia joined in, but still nothing happened.

"Oh no," moaned Ophelia. "I thought that once the person who caused the sleep was out of the house, the antidote spell would work. What's wrong?"

"Nothing," Mrs Wolf told her. "This spell never fails."

She tried again and again, but without success, until Ophelia was frantic.

"What are we going to do?" she wailed. "Gran is getting fainter all the time!"

Mrs Wolf hurried them back to the kitchen and began concocting a mixture in one of the pans that Mr Havelock had managed to clean out.

"What are you doing?" asked Waldorf.

"Making a drinkable anti-sleep potion," answered Mrs Wolf.

"You forgot the cinnamon," he told her.

"You know more than I thought you did," said Ophelia.

Waldorf brushed a paw over his face in embarrassment.

"Oh, he'll be the perfect familiar for you, Ophelia," muttered Mrs Wolf, shaking cinnamon into her mixture and tasting it.

They poured it, drop by drop, into Grandmother's mouth. But still nothing happened.

"I just don't believe it!" cried Mrs Wolf in exasperation.

"It can only mean that Mary is still in the house," said Mr Havelock from the doorway.

"But we saw her run off," argued Ophelia. "She couldn't have got back that quickly!"

"She's a witch, remember," said Mr Havelock. "She will have managed to hide herself somewhere in the house, so we're not able to rescue your grandmother in time. That way she'll have her revenge on you."

"We'll have to search the place from top to bottom," said Mrs Wolf, thinking fast, "and Ophelia, you must tell us which bits are really part of the house and which bits aren't."

They began immediately, Mrs Wolf displaying her thoroughness to an extraordinary degree as every door knob, light switch, cushion, button, curtain ring and ornament came under her scrutiny.

"I'm sure we would have heard her come in," sighed Ophelia.

"Not if she turned herself into a small animal or insect," replied Mrs Wolf, "before changing into a shape that would be even more difficult for us to find."

The search failed. Ophelia burst into tears and Mrs Wolf led her into the living room and sat her down on the sofa.

"Don't cry, my dear," she said rather hopelessly. "We'll do it all again in an hour or so."

But Ophelia wasn't listening to her. She was sitting very still and staring intently at the fireplace.

"What is it?" asked Mrs Wolf.

"Sssh, I think I hear something," whispered Ophelia.

They sat and listened. The noise that had caught Ophelia's attention was repeated: a gentle rustle coupled with a sad cry that sounded far away.

"There's something in the chimney!" cried Ophelia.

They called Mr Havelock and he poked up the chimney with a pair of tongs until he dislodged something. It fell into the fireplace with a squashy thud.

Ophelia stared in disappointment. There was no way the sooty, starving pigeon that sat before them now could be Mary.

They all took a closer look. The black-feathered lump tried to raise itself on to its legs but fell over again.

"It might be Mary," said Mr Havelock cautiously.

"It might," agreed Mrs Wolf, looking at the bird more closely.

"I think it's a perfectly harmless bird," said Ophelia, rather to their surprise. She scooped the bird into her hands and blew on it, sending a cloud of soot floating to the floor. "Look at it,"she said sadly. "It's half starved and one of its wings seems to be broken. It must have been up the chimney for hours. I'll take it to the kitchen to see if I can clean it up a bit."

Mrs Wolf and Mr Havelock looked at each other in dismay. Could Ophelia be right? Was the bird really as innocent as it looked?

Waldorf followed Ophelia. "Why don't you let Mrs Wolf try a little spell on it, just to make sure it's not Mary?" he begged, but she wouldn't hear of it.

She wiped the worst of the soot off the pigeon with a dirty cloth, then searched among the rubbish in the kitchen until she found what she was looking for. Mrs Wolf and Mr Havelock came to watch, still puzzled by Ophelia's behaviour. Ophelia lifted up the second of the gold cages in which Miss Walton had tried to imprison Mary and Blackie. It was badly battered and the gold was peeling but, nevertheless, it was in one piece.

"That's too small for a pigeon," Mr Havelock pointed out. "It's a canary cage." He stepped forward but Waldorf grabbed his trouser leg.

"I think she knows what she's doing," he told Mr Havelock.

Mr Havelock was right: the cage door was too small for a pigeon. But Ophelia picked up the bird and began to squeeze it through the doorway.

Suddenly, there was a flash of green light and Mary was sitting on the edge of the table with most of her skirt bunched up in the doorway of the battered cage. She no longer resembled Ophelia's grandmother.

"Pity you weren't quick enough to get me inside," she sneered.

"I would have had to break your neck to fit you in through that tiny doorway," Ophelia smiled. "And I would never have actually done it. If you hadn't changed back, I would have assumed I was wrong about you, and let you go."

Mary howled with rage at being tricked, and ripped her skirt as she pulled it out of the bird cage.

"I could have flown off by now!" she screeched. "I could have flown off and

157

returned as something else, to make sure your grandmother never woke up!"

Mrs Wolf and Mr Havelock stepped forward and Mary looked at them a little nervously. "What's the matter with you, Ophelia? Are you going to let these people fight your battles for you?"

Ophelia looked back at her steadily. "I'll fight you on my own," she said calmly.

Mrs Wolf and Mr Havelock begged her to let them help her, but Ophelia was adamant.

"You'll be able to step in if I need help," Ophelia told them firmly. "But Mary is right: this time, I should be fighting her myself."

For a moment, Ophelia and Mary faced each other across the room. Mary was rubbing her hands together, and as she rubbed, a ball of wool appeared and grew. Ophelia thought hard and the blue light glowed about her again. Mary shook out the wool between her hands with a flourish, and it became a sheepskin. She advanced towards Ophelia with a menacing look.

"Oh no," whispered Mrs Wolf. "She can withstand magic, but even the blue light can't protect her from physical violence!"

Mr Havelock had to grip her arm to prevent her interfering.

"Think of a dress," said Waldorf from down by Ophelia's knees.

Ophelia shut her eyes and thought of the dress in town that she had wanted so badly before Gran had her accident. It was black velvet with gold embroidery across the bodice and around the hem. Ophelia had noticed it on a dummy in the shop window, and thought it was the most beautiful thing she had ever seen; but Gran couldn't possibly afford it.

"I'm going to turn you into a sheep," said Mary with relish. "This is how familiars are made, you know."

But Ophelia didn't hear. She was thinking so hard about the black velvet dress with gold embroidery that she could actually see it in front of her. Now she could even reach out and touch it. She opened her eyes. At that moment, the sheepskin in Mary's hands turned into a black velvet dress with gold embroidery.

"Pah! Elementary tricks, my dear," spat Mary, tossing the dress aside.

"Rubbish," Mrs Wolf whispered. "That was actually very impressive!"

Mr Havelock nodded his agreement.

"So much for sheep," said Ophelia. "Now it's my turn." She wasn't quite sure what she was going to do, but she knew it had to be good. She

159

might not get a second chance.

She thought of her grandmother lying perfectly still in the room upstairs, night after night, while Mrs Wolf could do no more than dust her occasionally, and Mary took over the house. The more she concentrated the bigger the thought got.

Mary picked up a saucer from the table and said a few words over it. It grew larger, dripping gravy as it sprouted arms and legs. Mary set it down on the floor and it stalked slowly towards Ophelia, moving clumsily on its new legs. Ophelia didn't see it: she was thinking too hard about her grandmother's bedroom and its sleeping occupant.

"It's at times like this I feel so useless," croaked Mr Havelock, watching the advancing plate and shaking his spell-stuck hand in agitation.

"I'm not sure we should interfere yet," whispered Mrs Wolf hoarsely. She patted his hand and a brick flew from the end of his fingers, smashing the plate to pieces. The broken limbs withered away on the floor.

"You've unstuck my spells!" Mr Havelock grinned.

The room Ophelia was thinking of was still growing. Now she could see the bed quite clearly, as though she were standing in the room herself. But the bed was empty.

"I know," said Ophelia out loud. "Mary can live in it, just the way Gran has had to."

Mary started at the sound of Ophelia's voice. She couldn't see the room in Ophelia's imagination but she knew something was wrong. She gritted her teeth and thought of blue light, but her blue light wasn't natural, and it was tired from lack of use. It fell in tatters round her feet.

She threw a lizard spell at Ophelia, but it bounced off something in mid-air. Mary squinted: the spell hadn't even reached the girl before it fell to the floor. She cast an eye over their small audience and satisfied herself that they weren't helping. She didn't know, of course, that the spell had bounced off the walls of Ophelia's imaginary room.

She had to find out what Ophelia was concentrating so hard on, before she could destroy it. She strained her eyes in an attempt to see what Ophelia was looking at.

Now, I want Mary in my room, thought Ophelia.

By the time Mary saw the room in Ophelia's imagination it was too late. Having seen it, she knew she must be standing in it. So was Ophelia. Mrs Wolf and Mr Havelock had vanished.

Mary recognised the room as Grandmother's bedroom. Only Grandmother wasn't in it.

"There's no door!" she screamed at Ophelia.

"There's no window either," said Ophelia.

"How are we going to get out?" Mary

demanded. A chill was creeping through her bones now.

"I can get out quite easily," Ophelia smiled. "After all, we are in *my* imagination. As for you, you will have to get out the same way my grandmother did."

"But your grandmother hasn't got out yet, not out of the real room," protested Mary. Then she realised what Ophelia meant: she *wasn't going to get out.*

"You can't just trap someone in your imagination," Mary argued, trying to summon up her bravado.

"I can't say whether I can or not," replied Ophelia, feeling stronger than she'd ever felt in her life. "I can only do what comes naturally. After all, I'm a 'natural', remember?"

Mary seemed to be shrinking before Ophelia's very eyes, growing old and weak and tired.

"One last request," Mary pleaded. "Please, please, let me have my carpet bag."

Ophelia hesitated for a moment. Mary was bound to have an ulterior motive, and yet she couldn't think of one.

"I just want to have something of my own with me. Please, Ophelia. There's no way I can escape a room in your imagination, so let me have my one real possession with me."

163

Ophelia felt almost sorry for the fat, filthy woman before her, then she remembered her grandmother. No, even then, she couldn't be so cruel as to separate Mary from the one and only thing she owned. She looked at the empty bed and imagined the way the bag had looked the time she had searched through it. Then there it was, on the end of the bed.

"Oh, thank you; thank you," cried Mary, snatching up the bag and hugging it to her chest.

Ophelia thought of being in the kitchen again, and gradually the bedroom faded until all she could see was a shadow of it superimposed on the kitchen.

Mrs Wolf and Mr Havelock were clapping. "We've never seen anything like it!" they cried in unison.

"You were here all the time," said Mrs Wolf. "But Mary suddenly began to grow faint and indistinct. Then she was gone. What did you do with her?"

"I left her in a room with no doors and no windows somewhere in my imagination, I think," said Ophelia, collapsing into a chair.

"Well done, my dear," said Mrs Wolf, hugging her.

"I hope I did the right thing though," said

164

Ophelia.

"Of course you did," said Mr Havelock. "She only got what she so richly deserved. What ingenuity!"

"No, I hope I did the right thing when I left her with her carpet bag."

Mrs Wolf and Mr Havelock fell silent and looked at each other in dismay. "She will have all she needs in there," said Mrs Wolf slowly, "to perform the only spell that could rescue her from her situation."

There was a loud, disembodied laugh that echoed around the kitchen. "I'll be coming back!" shouted Mary's voice.

"What was in the bag, do you know?" asked Mrs Wolf urgently.

Ophelia told her about the bottles and tins and the little black book with the strange writing. Mrs Wolf sighed. "The spell for role reversal will be in her notebook. Every witch has it. It's too complicated to remember without notes, and now she has her notes."

"What's role reversal?" asked Ophelia curiously.

"That," said Mr Havelock, "is when one person swaps places and situations with another. The spell takes hours to prepare, which is why it's so rarely used, but now Mary

165

has all the time in the world."

"Aren't you forgetting something?" interrupted Waldorf.

Ophelia looked at him despairingly.

"*You* have her notebook," he said quietly.

"In the pocket of my old shirt," gasped Ophelia. "Yes, I'd forgotten."

Mary had obviously just made the same discovery. Her howl ripped through the air and died away. Then everything went quiet again.

Leaving Mrs Wolf and Mr Havelock to retrieve the Doctor from the excess foliage in the garden, Ophelia went upstairs with Waldorf. This time she wanted to see if she could wake Grandmother on her own.

She stood at the foot of the bed and said the anti-sleep spell that she now knew off by heart.

At first, nothing seemed to happen, then slowly, the old woman's breathing grew stronger and deeper. Ophelia watched with bated breath as the prostrate figure grew more dense and more vivid. The old lungs moved rhythmically and the eyes twitched beneath the eyelids, then struggled open, and Grandmother let out a rattling sigh.

"Gran," said Ophelia gently, "are you all right?"

The old eyes seemed to take a moment to focus on her, then Gran smiled. "Of course dear. Have you come to wake me? Is it morning already?"

She heaved herself into a sitting position and Ophelia sighed: it was going to be more difficult to explain than she had thought. Then she burst into tears.

"You've been asleep so long I thought you would never wake up," she cried.

"I think you'd better tell me all about it, don't you?" suggested Gran.

Ophelia looked at Waldorf.

"Perhaps *you* would explain it this time," she asked him.

Waldorf obliged. He recounted everything that had happened since he had arrived at the house, and any details he couldn't furnish Ophelia added.

"After all that," said Gran when he had finished, "the fact that you can talk is a minor observation."

She insisted Ophelia help her downstairs to see the mess. "I've missed all the excitement," she said, "so I might as well see what it looked like."

Ophelia helped her grandmother downstairs and was surprised when they were met in the kitchen by Mabel, Susannah and Rebecca. Then Mrs Wolf, the Doctor and Mr Havelock came in from the garden to join them.

"We came back to make sure everything was all right," explained Susannah. "We left Tracy helping Miss Wade to cover for us again."

Beatrice the chicken emerged from beneath the table and laid an egg.

"And while we're here," added Mabel, "we thought we'd clear this place up for you."

"I see you're looking more like yourself today, Doctor," Ophelia smiled.

Mrs Wolf threw her a warning glance, as much as to say "He doesn't know."

The Doctor grunted with embarrassment. "I can't remember what happened to me," he muttered, rubbing his forehead as if to massage his memory into action.

"I'm sure Mrs Wolf will tell you all you need to know," said Ophelia.

Mrs Wolf led her husband out to the car as quickly as possible, waving to Ophelia over her shoulder as she went.

There was nothing else for Ophelia, Mr Havelock and Gran to do, except watch the three girls clear up, magically mend things and create order from chaos. They refused to allow

Ophelia to help on the grounds that she had done more than her fair share already.

Then, just when everyone thought it was really over, there was a shadow at the broken kitchen window. For one awful moment Ophelia thought Mary might have escaped the imaginary room after all. But it was Miss Rose.

Mr Havelock and the girls went white as Miss Rose flew into the room and alighted in front of Susannah. Ophelia was about to beg forgiveness on behalf of the others, when Miss Rose bent down to pick up Beatrice.

"I'm sorry to disturb you, girls," she said, tucking the chicken firmly under her arm, "but I only came to pick up Beatrice. There's a chicken farm that is interested in her egg-laying." She turned to Gran. "I'm glad to see you looking so much better," she said genially, "and I hope we meet again when you bring Ophelia back to school. I shall expect the girls when I see them. I've told the cooks to keep their lunch warm." Then she turned on her heel and flew back out of the window.

"Well!" exclaimed Susannah. "I do believe she knew about this all the time! Mind you, they'll have to keep our supper warm too, at this rate, because even with magic, cleaning up is going to take all day."

"No it won't." Mr Havelock grinned. He put his hand in his pocket and pulled out one of the small, many-legged furry purple creatures he had lost on the classroom floor. "I found this just before I followed you here," he explained, "and while you might be able to clear up, none of you knows how to get rid of that mound of rubbish the way this little fellow can."

Gently, he set the tiny creature on the floor. "This animal will eat and eat," he told them, "and the more it eats the bigger it grows, and the bigger it grows, the hungrier it gets."

He was right. The little creature polished off the filth on the kitchen floor with its long and growing tongue, then emptied the overflowing dustbin, licked all the contents out of the saucepans and set to work on the corridor. It didn't even miss the rotting weeds in Mary's wardrobe. Ophelia only just managed to rescue the black velvet, gold-embroidered dress in time, or that would have been part of lunch too – and she wanted to keep it as a souvenir.

"This is wonderful!" she cried. "But how do you stop it?"

"You can't," said Mr Havelock, blushing. "I, er, thought it could be kept as a school pet."

"Never thinks first," muttered Mabel. "That's his trouble."

171

The purple thing was now the size of a baby rhino, and its legs, which hadn't quite grown in the same proportion, could barely support it.

"But it's getting too big!" called Ophelia.

"Bring it to me," said Gran.

Rebecca and Ophelia caught it by its tiny ears on the landing, where it had just finished chewing through an eiderdown, and led it downstairs. In its enthusiasm, the creature chewed their sleeves and tore at their clothing.

"Oh dear, I see what you mean," gasped Mr Havelock. "There was far more to eat than I imagined."

"It was probably the last bedspread," giggled Mabel.

"Look at me," said Gran sternly to the creature.

The animal, now sitting very still, stared up at her.

"You've done what you wanted to do, haven't you?" she asked it.

The creature nodded its whole body because it had no head.

"You've had enough to eat?"

The creature swung its body from side to side in an emphatic "No!"

"I told you so," sighed Mr Havelock.

"You've had enough to eat, haven't you?"

said Gran again.

This time the creature nodded.

"It's time to go home now, isn't it?" said Gran firmly.

The creature looked up at Mr Havelock sadly, and let out a moan from the depths of its belly.

"Couldn't we keep it, Gran?" asked Ophelia.

The old lady shook her head.

"Go home now," said Gran, bending over until her nose nearly touched the animal in front of her.

The creature backed away until it bumped into Mr Havelock. He bent down and began to push it and squeeze it, knead it, and squash it, and little by little the animal shrank. When it was back to its original size, Mr Havelock took it in his palms and rubbed it between them until it was a smooth ball, then he dropped it into his pocket.

He thanked Gran profusely. "There was no way I would ever have got him to let me do that without your help," he confessed.

Ophelia and Gran were sitting in the kitchen of their newly decorated house drinking tea.

"Everyone's been so wonderful," sighed Ophelia. "I've never had friends like Susannah,

Rebecca and Mabel before. Or even Tracy – though she's difficult, because you never know that she's there."

"You'll be seeing a lot more of them," Gran smiled.

Something outside the window caught Ophelia's eye. She followed Waldorf into the garden to have a closer look.

It was Blackie, finally coming down from the tree now that all was quiet. As soon as she saw Waldorf she climbed right back up again.

"I promise I won't hurt you," called Waldorf, "if you'll just come down from there."

Blackie waited a moment, then obviously decided she didn't want to stay up the tree for ever.

"What are you going to do now?" Ophelia asked her, not unkindly.

Blackie no longer looked a bit like her. She did look as though she had just spent the night in the back of a dustcart.

"Find another home, I suppose," mumbled Blackie faintly.

Waldorf vanished into the hedge on one side of the garden, and reappeared a moment later carrying what looked like a piece of material in his mouth.

He dropped it at Blackie's feet. "I think it

might be easier to find a new home if you're properly dressed," he said.

Blackie picked the material up and shook it out. Ophelia could see that it was a cat skin without the tail. (Blackie was still wearing her tail beneath her dress.) With a sigh of resignation, Blackie took off all but her underwear and climbed back into the skin, shrinking as she did so, until finally the head of the skin fitted over her face like a mask.

When she'd finished, Ophelia and Waldorf were staring at a skinny grey cat.

"She looks almost good enough to keep," commented Ophelia.

Waldorf threw her a warning glance and told

her to put the little silver wrist chain she wore round the cat's neck.

"It will stop her climbing out of her skin again," he explained. Then he suggested Blackie leave before he remembered how much he hated cats.

The cat was through the hedge and out of sight in a second.

"Will *you* ever climb out of your skin again?" asked Ophelia suddenly.

Waldorf lowered his head.

"I don't like to," he said.

"But why?"

"Because I prefer it if you just think of me as an unusual dog. Thinking of me as a human will only cause problems later," he told her. "Besides which, I'm *not* human."

"I suppose you'll go home now, wherever that is," said Ophelia sadly. It was something she had been dreading. "Isn't that what always happens when the baddies have been dealt with?"

Waldorf laughed out loud. "Yes," he said, "that is what happens. So I'll see you inside." With that, he padded back to the kitchen. "Don't be too long out here," he called over his shoulder. "We have to get an early night. It's school in the morning."